JOE AND KAY WEST NOVEL

FIGHT
TO
SURVIVE

Primix Publishing
East Brunswick Office Evolution
1 Tower Center Boulevard, Ste 1510
East Brunswick, NJ 08816
www.primixpublishing.com
Phone: 1-800-538-5788

Published by Primix Publishing: 11/05/2024

ISBN: 979-8-89194-318-6(sc)
ISBN: 979-8-89194-319-3(hc)
ISBN: 979-8-89194-320-9(e)

Library of Congress Control Number: 2024918698

Prologue

Randy moaned as he slowly became conscious. With being conscious came the pain. Slowly, his faculties started coming back. Realizing he was hanging from the ceiling.

His arms ached from being overextended.

There had been seven when they caught up with him. He had killed the first two immediately, then severely injured a few more. Although the numbers were not on his side, and between the remaining three, they had finally put him down. The last blow had knocked him out. It was that big guy. The one he had been trying to stay away from.

Trying to open his eyes, he realized one was nearly swollen shut. Slowly, moving only his eyes, he scanned the room. He looked to be alone. He could see his equipment lying on a desk about ten feet away. It might as well have been ten miles. With his hands bound and a hook between them, hanging from the ceiling, he was helpless.

Scared to tip his head for fear of passing out again, he tried to figure out how badly they had beat him. His right eye was getting worse and so were his arms. They felt like they were on fire. The muscles had been stretched by his body weight, although he thought he could feel the floor with the tips of his toes.

A short fat man walked in and slapped him hard several

times, asking questions in Spanish.

Randy replied, "I don't understand you," even though he understood every word.

The fat man walked over and picked up one of the knives. The man examined the knife as he walked back. The razor-sharp edge sparkling in the light.

Randy asked, "Hey you. What are you going to do with that?"

The man smiled as he answered in broken English. "I'm going to ask questions. If I think you lie to me. I cut you."

Randy kept scanning the room, looking for something.

Anything he could use to get free.

The fat man asked, "Did you blow up my manufacturing building?"

Randy replied, "What building? Where? When?"

The fat guy slapped him again and again. He stood back and drove his fist into Randy's stomach. Gasping for air, he hung there, beaten, and bloody. Randy could feel fresh blood flow from the older wounds on his face. The man walked behind him and slashed his back with a knife. Then he placed the blade between two of his ribs and slowly started to push.

Randy clamped his mouth shut so hard he thought he might break his teeth. It took everything he had hanging there, totally helpless, not to cry out. The pain was intense, although he didn't want to give this asshole the pleasure of knowing how much pain he was causing.

As the blade moved deeper, Randy thought, *He's going to puncture my lung and I'm going to drown in my own blood.*

Just then, he stopped and slowly pulled the knife out. The pain was almost unbearable. With his teeth clenched, he never uttered a word. Randy could now feel hot liquid running down his back. Trying to blank out the pain, he again started looking and thinking of a way to escape.

The fat man walked back in front of him and said, "Where did you get this knife and those pistols? Who do you work for? Where is your base camp? You answer me. I'll kill you quick. You continue to lie to me; you will die slowly."

Randy replied, "I'm a scientist. I work for the University of Virginia in partnership with the University of Colombia. The knives are mine, but I found the pistols on a dead body in the jungle."

Pablo slapped him and screamed, "Lies, all lies. This is a military knife. No one around here has silenced guns." He made two fast slices at Randy's chest.

Every muscle in his body became tense as he felt the pain from the two slashes. Clenching his teeth, he managed to say, "I'm telling you the truth. I found the guns. I'm a scientist. I'm here studying the wildlife."

Pablo glared and then started smiling as he walked away, turning and saying, "I'm going to enjoy killing you." He flashed the razor-sharp blade in the light.

As Pablo stepped forward, Randy quickly brought both feet up. Then kicked out with everything he had, connecting with the fat man, sending him crashing into the wall. As he swung back, he turned his head just enough to see a table. Hooking his feet under it, he pulled it forward. Letting it go, he swung forward and back again, getting his knees on it. Then raising his hands, he slipped the hook. He was now on his feet and had a chance at defending himself.

Pablo charged across the room, screaming like a banshee. Randy side stepped, charged, and dropped to one knee and swept the guy's legs as he passed by. As the man lost his balance and crashed into the table, Randy got to his feet, turning, and in a few quick steps, he was at the desk and his equipment. He grabbed the second knife and cut his hands loose, just as the fat guy started getting to his feet. Now armed with a knife, he looked at him and said, "I'm going to cut your throat and tear out your tongue and show you before you hit the ground."

The guy grabbed a chair, threw it at Randy, then ran out the nearby door screaming in Spanish that the prisoner was loose and he was escaping.

Randy grabbed his shirt and strapped on his belt, containing his pistols and ammunition. Then, looking for his MP5, he saw what looked like a first aid kit, along with a small day pack. Dumping the contents of the box into the pack, he headed for the door just as two guys came busting through.

Randy shot the first one in the center of his chest and knifed the second in the shoulder just below his collarbone as he ran past. Turning with the guy, he then swung the pistol like a hand axe connecting with the side of the man's head and watched as the man crumpled into a pile on the floor.

Taking a deep breath, he looked around and saw what he thought were his boots. Grabbing them, he saw his MP5 and grabbed that, too.

He then bolted out the other door and ran as hard as he could for the jungle, disappearing from sight.

Pausing for just a minute, he put the boots on and wiped the blood away the best he could. Throwing the first of his two shirts away, he worked his way deeper into the jungle and away from the compound.

Just before dark, he decided he needed to patch himself up and maybe try to get some rest. Opening the day pack, he found a bottle of hydrogen peroxide. Carefully, he poured part of the bottle down his chest. Then, taking a gauze, he covered the knife wounds on his chest. He poured the remaining contents of the bottle down his back. Taking more of the gauze, he tried to cover the two slices in his pack, plus the puncture wound. Looking into the pack again, he saw a pressure bandage.

This is for snake bites, he thought as he wrapped everything in place.

Afterwards, he decided to get farther away that night.

There was no doubt they were already after him or would be soon. Reaching in the fanny pack, he located his GPS. Pushing and holding the power switch, he waited for the unit to power up and then locate itself.

Looking at the screen, he was about thirty miles from his equipment stash and at least fifteen miles to the nearest city where he could possibly get help, although he was only twenty miles from Bogota and the US Embassy.

Pausing for a couple of minutes, he thought, *If I go north, then I'll circle all the way around before heading to Bogota. Hopefully, when they find my trail, they'll think I'm headed for Panama or Venezuela. Maybe they'll be too far behind, and I'll make it.*

Moving all night and until late the following afternoon, Randy finally had to stop and make a small camp. He figured he could sleep two hours and then go again. If everything went just a little bit right, he would be safe by about noon or so the next day.

As he rested, his memory cleared.

He had found the largest cocaine manufacturing compound he had ever seen in his ten years of being in Colombia. He only had eight phosphorus grenades left. Slowly, he circled the compound again. It was three in the morning. He had been watching the area since about noon the day before. He had spotted the guards earlier. They looked to have settled in for the night. *Now is the time*, he thought.

He made his way through the jungle to the backside of the last building. Slowly, he approached and brought his head high enough to look through the filthy window. Carefully, he tried to wipe them just a little so he could get a better view. Cussing under his breath, he realized the white film was on the inside. Quietly, he made his way to the rear door. As he thought, *I bet you get messed up just walking through there.*

Again, he raised himself just enough to see. The place looked to be empty. Bringing his suppressed MP5 submachine gun into position, he slowly opened the door and scanned the inside. The room looked to be about fifty feet long and maybe thirty feet wide. All his grenades had a five second fuse. He was sure he could throw five in that time.

"That should cause a fire that'll completely destroy this building and everything inside and really piss them off," he said out loud.

He knew he was about to kick over the largest hornet's nest ever.

The cartel would stop at nothing to hunt him down. Smiling, he slid the MP5 down and started placing the grenades on the table.

Picking up the first two, he pulled the pins and threw them one, two, as hard as he could towards the far end and opposite corners. With the first two still in the air, he grabbed two more. Pulling both pins, he threw them about half as hard. He tossed the last just as the first two went off, followed seconds later by the rest.

Instantly, the lights in the compound came on. With the building totally engulfed in flames, he ran for the safety of the jungle, pausing just a minute and looking back. People were running everywhere. It was total chaos. However, what caught his attention was a small group looking through binoculars, trying to locate him.

Chapter One

Kay and Joe stood holding each other in the pilot's room of the FBO, or fixed base operations, in a small airport in the heart of the Wrangell–St. Elias mountains of Southeast Alaska.

Kay is the managing editor for a large magazine based in Chicago, while Joe is a professional hunter. The two make an improbable couple to fall in love. Although fall in love, they do. They say opposites attract.

Today, they are waiting for the pilot to decide if he can get out of the valley.

The weather had them socked in, and the clouds had dropped dangerously low, with the visibility nearly nonexistent. Flying in Alaska was already dangerous, and these conditions made trying to fly even more dangerous.

Joe loved what he did. His job consisted of live trapping or hunting dangerous animals. He was in Alaska to track down and live-trap a grizzly that had started killing the livestock of the local ranchers. He had talked to the people who had seen or had trouble with the grizzly, or one eye, as some ranchers had started calling it.

Joe had spoken to a few guys who had seen the bear up close. Steve Davis, a local rancher, explained, "It's missing both an eye and an ear on the left side."

Joe replied, "It's probably an old male and was injured

in a fight over females. When those big bruins get to fighting during mating season, it can be brutal. Sometimes, one or both are severely injured." Looking around, Joe continues, "Grizzlies have a fantastic sense of smell. They can smell blood for miles. Next is their hearing, although their eyesight is poor. They can run close to thirty-five miles per hour for a short distance. You say he's big. Have you seen him standing on his rear legs?"

Steve answered, "Yes, I have, and I would put him somewhere between eight and nine feet tall."

Joe shook his head as he replied, "Wow, he is big. That would probably put his weight somewhere between eight and nine hundred pounds."

Dave Charles, another of the local ranchers, said, "I've also seen him, and he seems to be blond to light brown in color. I've only seen one other that color in this area."

As they stood there talking, Joe broke in by saying, "I'm sure it's a transient bear looking for easier forage."

Joe had hiked through the area every day, looking for a sign. After a long day hiking in the rough terrain, he would stop every evening at a local restaurant that ranches used often. Many nights, he would run into at least one and usually more.

They would always update him if they lost cattle or saw a bear. Although try as he might, the bear showed no type of pattern. He didn't spend any length of time around any particular ranch.

The more he learned about the bear, the more he was convinced that the injuries may have kept the bear from hunting its natural prey. Most bears, including grizzlies, are omnivores, meaning they eat meat and grasses, berries — pretty much everything. There is one exception to this. The polar bear is pretty much a carnivore, and they eat mostly meat for about eight months of the year.

Everyone in the valley was scared it could start attacking people next. That was why Joe was called. He was one of the best at tracking down the right animal. He always preferred to live trap and relocate when possible. Killing or destroying the animal was always the last choice. That was the biggest reason most governments or state agencies called Joe. With the number of hunting outfitters and guides trying to make a living combined with the rising cost of licenses and trophy fees, then add in the decline in some of the wildlife, capture and relocation was always better. It gives the breeding population a helping hand.

Kay absolutely loved her job, although being the managing editor was a high pressure, stressful position. She had worked her way up from the bottom.

Hard work and dedication had paid off. She had started with the magazine fifteen years before as an editor, and now she oversaw that department.

Joe and Kay had not seen each other for nearly two

months, and Kay decided enough was enough.

She contacted Joe and had flown in two weeks earlier. Together, they had been hiking and camping, along with sightseeing and just being together, enjoying each other's company and this beautiful area of Southeast Alaska.

They had spent time doing almost everything, from sitting and watching the wildlife to hiking into high mountain meadows to enjoying the natural beauty of this area.

With some minor rock climbing, they had climbed to vantage points where they had seen moose, grizzlies, sheep, and caribou. The wildlife in Alaska is second only to its natural beauty.

As hard as it was, today was the last day, and she had to leave Joe and this beautiful area to return to Chicago along with the rat race of a high-pressure job of being a managing editor. Going back to that mess was not at the top of her priority list, and leaving Joe was the last thing she wanted to do. She knew his job was highly dangerous. All the animals he dealt with were deadly, along with the fact that most of them could injure or possibly kill him at any time. That thought was always in the back of her mind, so every minute they were together was a bonus.

Chapter Two

They met two years earlier at a party. Joe watched her walk in from across the room. It was instant. He had to meet her. She was absolutely beautiful. In his heart, without ever talking to her, he just knew she was the one.

As the evening progressed, he slowly worked his way toward where that beautiful lady was talking with a few guys and their wives or dates.

As he worked his way toward her, he stopped and talked to people he knew while never letting her out of his sight.

She had noticed him also. It was instant butterflies. She knew without a doubt he was someone special. Tall, well-built, and had those rugged good looks that she so adored.

As Joe approached where she was standing, he stopped to talk with another guy for a minute before turning and saying hello to her and offering his hand. The second their hands touched, something happened; they felt a spontaneous connection and affection for each other.

They talked for just a few minutes and that was it. They both knew there was no other. They had to be together. Nothing or no one else mattered. As he worked his way towards other people he knew, Joe had made a decision. Finding a pen and a napkin, he wrote his phone number on it. Folding it, he found his date and then spotted Kay. As he walked past her, he slipped a folded piece of paper into her hand.

Looking around for only a second, he saw the door and went out. Joe and his date left the party.

On the car ride back to town, all he could do was think of Kay. Arriving at his date's home, he walked her to the door, kissing her, he said, "Thank you, Desire. I had a great time."

She replied, "So did I. Would you like to come in for a drink?"

Joe looked at his watch and said, "I have to get packed to leave. Tomorrow, I'm shipping some equipment and I'm flying out later tomorrow or the following morning, although I should be back in a few weeks. Maybe next time."

Slowly, he drove back to the motel. Laying on the bed, he pictured Kay in his mind. *Wow, she is beautiful*, he thought. A woman like that could almost make him want to give up the outdoors.

The following morning, as his eyes flickered open, his first thought was Kay. He pictured her standing there. Red V-necked sweater and black skirt. Although the memory that kept coming back was the smile in her eyes as she said hi. Joe closed his eyes and could picture those beautiful eyes with that smile.

While in the shower, he thought he heard his phone. Quickly, he grabbed a towel and wrapping it around himself, he found his phone. A smile broke out as he listened to his voicemail.

Kay had called and left a message, saying simply, "This is Kay, the lady you met at the party last night." He couldn't believe it. She had called. Taking a deep breath, he pushed the call back.

Kay answered on the second ring, saying, "Good morning."

Joe replied, "Good morning, sunshine."

They talked for a few minutes and made plans to meet at a small café about three miles from his motel later that day.

Joe finished shaving, then, looking at himself in the mirror, he said, "Hello, Randal Jackson." That life seemed so long ago and so far away.

Could he actually have a somewhat normal life? The plastic surgeon had done a fantastic job of changing his appearance.

Getting dressed, he found the old picture he kept. He compared it to the man he saw in the mirror. That life and that man were gone after four years in Afghanistan, all in the mountains. On a continuous search and destroy mission, followed by ten years in Colombia. All black ops were spying on the Colombian drug cartel and not just drugs, but the cocaine cartel. Joe once again looked at the picture. That man was dead. He had died in the mountains of Afghanistan and then the jungles of Colombia.

After basic training or boot camp, he tested for Special

Forces training, which included paratroopers jump school. The training was brutal, but he was determined to be at the top of his class. After completing and graduating number one, an instructor asked him to test for sniper training. That was the easiest training he had. Randy had grown up hunting and was an excellent shot. Sniper's school just tweaked his natural ability. He had been shooting for years, both long-range and shorter targets.

Smiling, he thought of the survival training. He knew more about surviving in the mountains than the instructors did and showed them things they didn't think were possible.

He had spent years in the mountains. He also loved to hunt and had shot deer where they slept, never waking up. Not just deer, but big white tail bucks that are amongst the most skittish of the deer family. One year, after Randy had shot the second of two really nice bucks while they slept, his dad had said, "You are like the wind in the woods. Never making a sound that would alert anyone or anything."

After training, he volunteered for a mission in Afghanistan. Going through the equipment the army wanted him to carry, he started sorting. As the piles grew, Sergeant Colton asked, "What are you doing? That's government issued equipment."

Randy looked at him and replied, "I'm sure it is, and I'm sure it's all really good, although it's my ass over there, and I know what I want and need. I'll find what I'll bring, and you can do whatever you want with the rest."

Getting up, he continued, "Let's go to the armory. I need to find a certain rifle, a couple of pistols, and two knives."

The two men walked to the armory where Randy picked two six-inch MK3 naval knives. A 1911 Kimber .45 and a smaller H&K, both with threaded barrels. Grabbing four tactical suppressors, he then headed for the sniper rifles. Looking around, he walked past all the auto and semi-automatic rifles until he found a Remington Model 700 in 7.62 or .308, as most people know it. Taking three, they then headed for the rifle range.

Sergeant Colton watched with amazement. He would pick a target and Randy would put a hole in it. A little over an hour later, he had the one he wanted. Six shots in a three-inch group at four hundred yards. Randy explained most guns could shoot a three-shot group at most any range. It's what they can do after the barrels start to get warm that counts. Looking at Sergeant Colton, he asked, "Can you have the barrel of this threaded to take a suppressor?"

The sergeant replied, "Why a suppressor? And are you going to bring a close fighting rifle? Oh, and how many of these long-range guns do you want?"

Randy smiled and replied, "Silence is deadly. If they can't hear the shot, they'll have a hard time locating me. The longer I can stay undercover, the longer I can shoot and the more of those goat herders get to meet Allah."

Randy looks at the rifles and says, "In the coming days, I'll spend hours shooting. I'll find at least two more and, hopefully, three. I'll also want a couple of H and K MP5s and two M14 in 5.56 so that way, I can fire their ammunition as well as my own."

Sergeant Colton asked, "How much will you carry with you? I know you're in good shape. But you can't carry all that."

Randy answered, "Once I'm in the country, I'll find a supply drop high in the mountains. There, I'll keep all my extra guns, ammunition and whatever else I bring. It will depend on my orders. All I'll carry on patrol is one rifle, one of the MP5s, both pistols and both knives.

Sergeant Colton reached into his breast pocket and handed Randy an envelope. As Randy read, he snapped to attention and said, "Anything you need sir, just ask. I've been told to help you get ready to deploy."

The envelope contained Randy's orders and new rank. He was now Commander Randal Jackson. This would allow him to move freely between the fire bases and get whatever supplies he needed for his mission without the regular red tape that went with most military bases.

Next came the pistol range. It was a walk-through range with pop-up targets that were either friend or foe. Randy scored nearly perfectly. Just a little slow on a couple. The way it was set up was you had to decide in a matter of seconds if the gun they carried was pointed at you or not. You couldn't shoot at the ones not pointed at you.

Sergeant Colton whispered, "If they have a gun, shoot, and let God sort it out. Randy started laughing as the Sergeant continued, "Only kidding. Just be careful, you have signed up for the most dangerous mission we have."

Randy replied, "Yes, I know. But it's what I'm good at. I have spent my entire life hunting and in the mountains. I think it's time we put the fear of God into those goat herding assholes."

Over the next couple of months, Randy continued to train. He was given a half-hour head start. Then a couple of Army Rangers would try to find him. At first, it took them a few hours. As the training continued, it would take them all day. Towards the end, they would never find him. More than once, he would do a simulated ambush of the squad trying, killing, or wounding several. He has given the nickname the 'ghost'.

The last week of his training was the ultimate test. He was to evade three squads of Rangers, a squad of Navy Seals, and a squad of Army Special Forces with dogs for three days. In the simulation, he ambushed sniper style and killed several and then would simply melt back into the forest.

He told Sergeant Colton the night after the exercise was over, "You were within ten feet of me. I watched as you sat on the cliff and glassed the valley below. I was going to come up from behind, but then the rest of your squad showed up.

So, I sat and listened to your plans and backed out. I went southeast over the next mountain."

Sergeant Colton asked, "How do I know you were that close?"

Randy simply smiled and said, "You took a leak in the bushes about ten feet back from the cliff edge and when the rest showed up, you asked, 'Have any of you seen anything or have an idea where the hell he is?'"

Sergeant Colton swore under his breath as he announced, "He's right. That is exactly what happened." Then, looking back at Randy, he asked, "Did you move before or after we left?"

Randy replied, "I backed out while everyone walked around the cliff edge. You made more than enough noise to cover me crawling out. As soon as I couldn't hear you, I got up and walked away. I sat on the mountain to your east and watched as you headed northwest into the valley."

Sergeant Colton shook his head and said, "I think you're ready. I feel sorry for those Taliban assholes. They have no idea what's coming their way."

Joe shook his head, trying to clear the past as his thoughts came back to the present. Who was he trying to kid? His previous life would catch up with him again.

Standing, he walked into the bathroom and removed his shirt. He turned around and, looking in the mirror, he could see the scars they made as they slashed and then knifed him in the back. Turning to see the scars and bullet holes on his chest, he thought, *I can't meet her. If we ever got together and they find me, they'll kill her, too.* A tear started down his cheek. *Or something worse.*

Sitting there, he watched the clock and swore it was broken. Time stood still. Several times he got up and looked closer, making sure the second hand was actually moving. "My God," he said out loud, "Why am I so nervous? She's only a woman. Maybe the most beautiful woman I've ever met. But still a woman. I've met other women, but I've never acted or felt like this."

Letting his mind drift off again, he looked through the scope and watched as the guy hit that young child over and over. Moving the range finder into place, he got the yardage. Four hundred fifty-two yards. Just over a quarter mile. Making the adjustments, he moved his finger to the trigger once again. The man was on the list of known terrorists. Watching, he saw a woman run out. Abdul spun around and punched her, knocking her to the ground. Walking around, he then kicked her several times. The child ran to his mother's side just to be picked up and thrown against the wall. That was the last straw. Joe's finger slid onto the trigger once again.

He knew when he touched the trigger, it would be time to find a new area to work. He could come back here in a month or so. Taking a deep breath and releasing half, he placed the crosshairs just above his ear and applied a slow, light pressure.

A pink mist sprayed the wall behind Abdul as the 122-grain boat tail hollow point found its target. Abdul was slammed against the wall and crumpled to the ground with the right side of his skull missing. The woman looked around, grabbing her child as she ran into the nearby hut.

Chapter Three

J oe continued to think of his past.

After the military, he went to work for the DEA with his military training. He volunteered for a black ops mission into the jungles of Colombia. He gathered more intel on the Colombian drug cartel than any agent in history. Spending ten years as a deep cover agent, he handled almost all the drug information. This information led to arrests.

More importantly, he helped start the fighting between the cartels; the bloody wars that slowed the production and then the amount of cocaine being smuggled into the United States.

Joe shook his head. He wasn't Randal Jackson anymore. That guy was dead. He had died in the jungles of Colombia. The government had placed him in the witness protection program. A program designed to protect federal witnesses and retired agents who were wanted by the various drug cartels.

A year later, as he lay in bed, he heard something. Slowly, he rose, listened, and watched. There was someone moving into his apartment. They had found him. But how? That was supposed to be impossible. His name was Robert Easton at that time.

Slowly, he slid out of bed and placed two pillows where

he had been lying. Picking up his silenced .45 and walking quietly to the door, he stood so the door would cover him when they opened it.

The door flew open; the two men opened fire, shooting the pillows several times. Robert stepped out and put two slugs in the center of each of their chests.

Quickly, he gathered his belongings and left. He knew he could never trust anyone again, including the government. "Witness protection, my ass," he said as he left. His life would never be the same.

The following morning, Robert called his handler and reported what had happened, and said, "You have a mess to clean up. I'm gone. I don't want your help. Don't look for me. If you do, someone will have to clean up another mess. I don't trust you or anyone connected with your program."

Next, Robert contacted the one guy he knew he could trust. He called the DEA branch he was with and said, "Can I speak with Adrian Sawyer, please."

The receptionist replied, "Can I tell him who's calling."

"Yeah, tell him Randal Jackson," Robert said.

A few seconds later, Adrian answered, saying, "I haven't heard that name in a few years. How are you doing?"

Robert replied, "I'm in trouble. My cover has been blown. I killed two guys last night after they killed my pillows."

Adrian replied, "Aww, shit. Where are you? I'll have someone pick you up and bring you to me. We will start over and this time, do it right."

Robert replied, "No, not right now. I'll contact you in a couple of days. I'll tell you what I want, and you can send it. Right now, I'm running, and I don't trust anyone but you."

Joe sat up and looked around. That had been six years ago. A few days later, he made that call, he said, "I'll be in your office in three days. I trust you and only you. Between the two of us and one federal judge, we can get this done. Do you know one we can meet with? Just you and I?"

Adrian's reply was instant. "Yes, I do. It's the one we use for federal warrants. I'm sure we can trust him, and he'll know how

to set this up. I'll meet with him before you get here. Hopefully, by the time you get here, he'll have it done or nearly done."

Three days later, Robert walked up to a federal building in Washington, DC. Before 8 a.m.

Looking around, he saw a line of benches where he could sit and watch while still being out of a direct path.

Sitting down, Robert started to watch as people walked in to start their day. Soon, a large, powerfully built black man walked up. Robert got up and immediately blended into the crowd. Coming up from behind, he pushed the barrel of his .45 into his back and said, "You are getting sloppy." The man froze as Robert continued, "I think way too much time behind a desk."

Slowly, Adrian turned and looked into the eyes of a DEA living legend. The man who put his life on the line for the people of the United States every day without them ever knowing a thing about him or what he had done.

Sticking out his hand, Adrian said, "God, it's good to see you. It's been what over two years?"

Robert replied, "Yeah, at least. I've been sitting over there for a couple of hours. I've watched every guy that came near here, although I recognized you immediately."

Stepping back, Adrian replied, "You've changed. I don't think I would have recognized you."

The two men walked back to the bench, and sitting down, they talked about the old days—Colombia and Afghanistan that span the previous 15 years and nearly all of Randy's adult life.

A couple of hours later, he followed Adrian into the federal building to meet with federal judge, Wallace Fisher. In a matter of minutes, it was done. He had set up a completely new identity. By setting it up under the Patriot Act, he could use numbers for things like identification, bank accounts, and banks. Once entered into the federal computer system, all paperwork would come back to him. He would destroy all copies.

Handing Robert a sealed envelope, he said, "Here is your new identity. I'm the only one who knows what's in that envelope and that name. I think it would be a good idea to tell

Adrian. You may need a friend on the inside again someday, although that's entirely up to you."

Randy reached out and shook Judge Fisher's hand, saying, "Thank you, sir. Hopefully, this time, it works."

Judge Fisher replied, "It should. I buried that so deep in red tape and dead ends. I don't think I could ever get to the true name again."

Randy smiled as he said, "Thank you again, sir."

Together, the two men walked out of the building and Robert opened the envelope. Looking through the paperwork, he turned to Adrian and stuck out his hand. "Hi, I'm Joe West."

Taking the offered hand, he said, "Glad to meet you, Joe."

Joe took out a new cell phone and dialed a number. Adrian looked at his phone as Joe said, "Keep that number safe. Only you and that judge have it."

Adrian shook Joe's hand one more time and said, "Absolutely. Good luck, umm, Joe."

Turning, the two men walked in separate directions.

Chapter Four

Joe shook his head again, trying to clear the past.

Six years ago.

With only fifteen minutes before their meeting time, Joe slid a silenced 9mm Glock in his boot holster and pulled his jeans down to cover it. After a quick look in the mirror, he turned, locking the door as he headed toward the restaurant.

Arriving, Joe sat in his pickup and watched as people came and went. He looked at everyone and at every vehicle in the parking lot and surrounding area. Certain that no one was waiting in a nearby car, he finally went in.

As he entered, he looked around and saw Kay. Sitting in a corner booth with a cup of coffee and the most beautiful smile Joe had ever seen.

Joe's smile grew as he got closer and, taking her hand in a light handshake, he said, "I'm so happy you called. I was hoping you would while being scared to death you wouldn't."

Kay started laughing as she replied, "I felt the note slide into my hand. I didn't have any pockets in that outfit and my purse was outside in the car. So, I excused myself and went to the restroom. After reading it, I put it in my bra."

Joe was just taking a sip of coffee as she said that. It was unavoidable. He started laughing and tried to cover his mouth before spraying coffee everywhere.

Their conversation continued for the next several hours. They had dinner together and walked to a small bar, where they found a corner table. After having a couple of beers, they talked until nearly midnight.

Someone started the jukebox, and Joe reached for Kay's hand, and slowly, they started dancing. Just a slow circle as they talked. Neither of them was willing to take their eyes off the other. Finally, about two in the morning, they walked back to their cars.

Joe put his arms around Kay. The goodnight kiss lasted and lasted. They didn't want to let the other go. Finally, Kay asked, "How long will you be around here?"

Joe replied, "I'm flying out tomorrow." Looking at his watch, he said, "Make that today, although I should be back in a couple of weeks, maybe slightly longer. Can I see you when I get back?"

Kay's smile could have brightened the daylight. Although not wanting to sound too eager, she said, "I'm sure we can make that happen."

Joe laughed as he looked around and said, "I'll call you when I land. If my phone works up in the mountains or I can find a place with service, I'll call a few more times and when I'm done and headed back."

Kay asked, "What are you going to be doing?"

Joe replied, "There's a college that wants a couple of

wolverines. They have all the necessary paperwork. They hired me to live trap them and get them back East. They want a male and female so hopefully, I can locate capture and ship two in a couple of weeks or so. With a little luck, it won't take that long."

Kay asked, "Wolverines? Aren't they dangerous?"

"Not really," replied Joe. "Although they can really mess up your day if you are not careful. Adult males weigh anywhere from 40 to 60 pounds and have a nasty attitude. Females are about half that size but have the same attitude. Humans are not on their normal diet. Although there are a few cases where they have attacked. Usually, that's after someone has provoked them."

Kay smiled as she asked, "You really do love what you do. Don't you."

Joe smiled. He said, "If you love what you do. You'll never work another day of your life. Yes, I have the greatest job in the world. I make a good living doing what I love. I spend almost every day in the mountains or forest working with animals."

Kay wrapped her arms around him. Holding him close, she could feel the man she had been searching for her entire life. Giving him one more hug, she said, "Please be careful. I really do want to see you again.

Joe stooped down and kissed her as he replied. "Absolutely. I want to see you again."

Slowly, they let go of each other and headed in their separate directions.

Kay stood about five foot three with jet-black hair and the most beautiful eyes Joe had ever seen. Her personality was fun-loving and playful. When they were together, they laughed, joked, and teased each other. Everyone could see the way they looked at each other and what that look meant. She was very athletic and had a fantastic body. She also had a great love for the outdoors. She loved most anything and everything she could do outdoors. Although she was 100 percent woman; she looked fantastic dressed up for a dinner party.

Joe was an inch over six feet and a shade over two hundred pounds, with dark-blond hair and that outdoorsy build. He could walk all day in almost any type of terrain, from the forested areas of the Central United States to the rugged mountains of Alaska.

His love of the outdoors started as a young boy when he would wander for hours in the woods and mountains of Central Pennsylvania, where he grew up. He also loved everything outdoors, from hunting and camping to winter-survival camping.

Chapter Five

Joe pushed the throttles forward as the Cessna 310 gained speed. He eased back on the yoke as the plane lifted off the runway and started to climb. After opening his flight plan, he let out his breath and relaxed. He was headed back to the Chicago area, although more importantly, he was headed back to see Kay. He had been gone nearly a month. They had talked on the phone a few times. Although there was poor service where he had been, so the calls were scattered and short.

Picking up his cell, he touched Kay's name. Flipping a switch, connecting his phone to the plane's radio so he could talk to her through his headset.

A few rings later, Kay answered, saying, "Please tell me you're done out there and headed back here."

Joe replied, "Yes, ma'am. Just passing through one zero thousand and still climbing. I should be at the midway airport around six. Want to go out to dinner?"

Kay replied, "Nope, I'll cook you dinner. What time do you think you'll be at the house?"

Joe smiled. "For a home-cooked meal, say six-thirty to seven. Sooner if I land on the road going past your driveway."

Kay laughs as she says, "I don't think that's a good idea. What would the neighbors think?"

Joe laughed. "They would think I missed you."

"Do you miss me?"

Joe smiled as he thought about the last month. "Absolutely every day."

Reaching, Joe eased the throttles forward just a bit more. Readjusting the props and taking a glance at the rest of the gauges and instruments, he said, "I'll call you if I hit or have to go around any bad weather; oh, and when I'm about an hour away from the airport. That'll give me a better idea of what time I'll be giving you a hello kiss."

Kay smiled as she thought about the last several months. Every time she had hugged him, she could feel the man she had been looking for. The smile grew as she replied, "I missed you, too. See you around seven."

***

Pulling into the driveway, Joe shut off the pickup and let out his breath. How could he miss a lady he's only known a few months? Knocking on the door, Kay opened it and reached for the man reaching for her. The kiss should have been R-rated as their tongues started a dance they would both remember. Breaking the kiss, Joe's mouth moved to her neck and back to her lips, and Kay responded like she was in love.

Taking Joe by the hand, she pulled him inside and closed the door. Turning, she saw Joe standing there with one of the biggest smiles and an ever-larger bouquet of roses. Taking the flowers, she led him into the house. Joe had only been there once and for just a few minutes. Kay showed him around and pointed down the hall. "The master bedroom and bath are down there."

Joe saw the fireplace and asked, "Does your fireplace work?"

"Absolutely."

Joe asked, "Would you like a fire?"

"Oh, please. There's some wood next to it and more stacked behind the garage."

Joe headed for the back door with the wood holder. Seeing the woodpile, he picked eight nice pieces of oak. Then, looking around, he saw the axe. He placed one more piece on top of another; he split it into several smaller pieces and placed that on top of what he'd already got. Walking back into the house, he had a fire going in a few minutes.

Kay called from the kitchen. "There are a few of those fire logs in the closet. I use them to get the fire going." As she walked into the living room, a nice fire was already burning. "How did you get that going that fast?"

"Sometimes, when I'm working, I need a fire, and I need it now. Like if it's winter and I get wet. I've learned over the years how to get one started and make it keep burning. At times, my life could depend on it."

Kay walked up to Joe, wrapping her arms around him. "Well, when we go camping, you can be in charge of always getting the fire started. There are times I couldn't keep one going with five gallons of gas and a blow torch."

Joe laughed. Holding her close, he kissed her and said, "Oh wow. Okay, I'll light the campfire, along with also keeping a fire going in you."

Kay replied with a seductive smile. "You won't need gas for that. You already got a small one started."

Joe smiled and pulled her a little closer. Bending forward, he gave her a very romantic kiss.

"Every one of those will help it burn just a little bigger and brighter."

Joe pulled her in close again. "Come here. I want to start a forest fire." As their tongues touched, a romantic waltz started again.

Kay let out her breath as they separate and quietly said, "I think it's already started." As she headed back to the kitchen, she picked up a plate with two hand-cut rib-eye steaks. She then asked, "Do you like to cook on a grill?"

Joe took the steaks and said, "Point me to your grill." Stopping, he looked at the steaks and asked, "Do you have any Prime Rib rub?"

Kay opened a cupboard and said, "Absolutely," as she handed the container to him.

Taking the container, Joe moved one steak and shook a generous amount on both. Turning them over, he repeated the process. Looking at Kay, he asked, "Ready now, where's the grill?"

"It's on the patio by the woodpile. It's a new pellet type. Follow me; I'll help you get it started."

Together, they walked out the back door. Joe looked at the grill and turned the temperature knob to four hundred degrees. Closing the lid just as Kay came back out with a couple of bottles of beer.

Joe watched as the temperature climbed as Kay asked, "Are you going to put the steaks on?"

"Yep, just as soon as that temperature gauge is over 400." Looking inside, he slid the heat shield back to expose the flame. Taking the two steaks, he placed one directly on top of the flame for a minute or so before flipping it to the other side then sliding it away from the heat; he repeated the process with the other steak. Then, sliding the heat shield closed, he asks, "How do you like your steak cooked?"

Kay took a sip of her beer. "Medium well to well. A little pink is okay, just no blood, please."

Joe walked back to the grill and slid one steak directly above the heat, but leaving the shield closed as he looked at his watch. Sitting down, he picked up his beer. "About ten minutes and you'll be biting into the best steak you've ever had."

Kay said, "I'll be right back. I'm going to check the rest of dinner."

Joe stood as Kay got up and headed back into the house, only to reappear in a couple of minutes with two more beers.

"Everything is ready, just waiting on you and them." She nodded at the grill.

Joe looked at his watch.

Getting up, he headed to the grill to flip both steaks. Glancing back at Kay, he said, "They are ready."

Kay walked in, bringing out two plates a few minutes later. The plates were loaded with twice-baked potatoes and French-cut green beans.

Sitting on the patio, Joe opened a bottle of wine as they got ready to eat. They talked about the upcoming hunting season and the fact that he would be gone from mid-September to the middle of November, depending on snowfall in western Montana.

Kay sliced off the first piece. After swallowing, she said, "Wow, this is perfectly cooked, and still juicy and delicious."

Joe smiled. "The way that grill is designed, it can sear a steak. Then by closing the heat shield, it cooks without drying them out. I've heard of that kind of grill, although I've never seen one until now. It's also a smoker. Someday, we can do ribs. I bet they'll be just as good."

"I bet they would be superb. So, you'll be gone nearly three months?"

Joe chewed and swallowed, taking a sip of wine. "Yeah, sorry, but during that time, I'll make nearly $30,000, and that's a nice bonus before winter sets in and I stay home until April or May."

With supper done, Joe helped Kay do the dishes and clean up the kitchen. Then, taking her by the hand and with the bottle of wine, they walked into the living room to sit down and enjoy the fire.

Kay reached over and turned on some music. Talking and listening together, they enjoy a few quiet minutes. As the song ended and another started, Joe took Kay's hand and slowly they danced.

Joe kissed her as they turned a slow circle. As the song ended, they continued to kiss as they slowly walked backwards toward the couch.

Slowly and carefully, he laid her down on the couch as his hands explored her body. Kay's breathing deepened as he found her places of pleasure.

Kissing his way down her neck, he slowly unbuttoned her blouse. Unhooking her bra, he kissed his way between her breasts and slowly kissed his way over to a nipple. Tenderly, he bit, then sucked one, then the other as his hands continued to explore her beautiful body.

While still kissing and sucking on her nipples, his hands found their way up and under her dress. Her breath came in gasps as his fingers found more places of pleasure.

Kay's hands start to explore also. Finding a certain place, she continued to rub and then got his pants unsnapped. Sitting up, she took him by the hand while still kissing. They weave and bounce their way to the bedroom wherein a few minutes, they're both stripping away clothing and are on the bed.

Joe paid more attention to her breast, then slowly, he kissed his way down her stomach. Stopping at her belly button, he kissed a circle around it, then slowly kissed his way farther down.

Kissing the inside of her thighs, he lifted her leg and kissed her calves, then the inside and back of her knee and up the inside of her thighs. Changing back and forth until he reached her pubic mound, kissing a circle around it. He flicked his tongue back and forth until he found what he was looking for. Then slowly, he licked, kissed, and softly sucked as Kay's movements told him he was there.

She felt the first wave as it grew, building and building until it broke with a body-trembling climax. She cried out, "Oh, God. Yes, yes," as the second wave started as soon as the first slowed. As the second built, Joe continued doing the soft sucking, and the wave broke stronger and harder than the first. Again, Kay cried out, "Oh God, yes."

Grabbing Joe's head and holding him in place, the waves continued to build and break. Kay softly moaned until one started and built, rolls and builds, higher and higher. Then, with an explosion, it broke. Kay cried out again and again, "Oh God, y es. Oh God, oh God." Joe slowly started kissing his way back up. Stopping at her breast, he softly bit and sucked. While he slowly eased his way inside her, in and out faster and faster. Kay met every thrust in perfect harmony. Together, they reached that explosive point of no return. Kay cried out again, "Oh God. Oh God. Yes, yes, yes." Another wave broke as Joe released.

Together, they slowed down.

Kay wrapped her legs around him, holding him in place as their lips and tongues found each other, starting another slow, loving dance. Finally, Joe rolled to the side, breathing deeply as Kay rolled onto her side. Joe pulled her closer and held her tight.

Kay whispered, "Oh my God. I think I've forgotten how great sex can be, and I don't think I've ever climaxed that many times."

Joe smiled. "That's not sex. That, my dear, is making love, and you're right, I had forgotten also. Oh, and by the way, my name is Joe, not God. But thanks for the great compliment. I'll take being compared to him in any way and all day."

Kay laughed and gave him a tender bite on his neck before getting up. Walking to the closet, she took out a sheer black silk robe. Putting it on, she turned to Joe and said, "Grab the wine, and I'll meet you in the living room."

Joe slipped on a t-shirt and sweatpants, then grabbed the bottle and both glasses, and headed for the living room. Opening the fireplace, he stirred up the coals, dropped in a few smaller pieces and one nice piece of oak. In just a few minutes, the fire was blazing just as Kay walked in, smiled, and said, "Wow, that's three nice fires you've started tonight." Then, smiling very seductively, she said, "Want to continue working on the second one a while longer?"

Joe closed the fireplace doors; standing up and filling both wine glasses, he turned, handing one to Kay. She took a sip and put hers down.

Joe reached for her, and pulling her close, he kissed her. Some of the wine was still on her tongue as he sucked it into his mouth.

Sitting down, he slowly opened her robe just a little and carefully poured some between her breasts. Then, kissing and licking his way between her breasts, Kay's breathing came in short gasps.

Joe reached over and took an ice cube into his mouth. Carefully, he placed it between his teeth and started slowly moving it across her bare skin, causing her to tremble. Opening her robe a little more, he drew the ice cube across her nipples and watched as the nipple expanded and grew. Then slowly down her belly, leaving it in her navel. Slowly, he kissed his way back up to her breast, kissing and tenderly biting. He then slowly worked his way back down and sucked the melted water and ice cube back into his mouth, and slowly drew it again across her bare skin up to her neck and lips, where he started again to kiss her.

Reaching down, Kay took him in her hand and slowly stroked him as she stood. Joe's lips found hers, and still holding him in her hand, she again walked on shaking legs, bouncing off the walls as they continued to kiss their way back to the bedroom.

Chapter Six

Joe awoke with a start. His training kicked in, and he laid perfectly still. Something had just moved, but what? Now wide awake, he listened. Slowly, his hand slid sideways and found a warm body next to his. Pausing, he slowly turned his head to see Kay lying on her side. He let out his breath.

Wow, it was just her turning in her sleep.

Reaching over, he put his arm around her and slid her closer. Kissing her neck, he thought, *I need to learn how to sleep with someone. Thank God I know that I have to lie still until I can tell what's going on and if it's dangerous or not.*

Joe's internal alarm goes off at five-thirty. The same time every day.

Slowly, he slid out of bed and, pulling on a t-shirt and sweatpants, headed for the kitchen. Making a pot of coffee, he poured two cups and walked back into the bedroom. Carefully, he placed one close to Kay as he sat looking at the woman he had just woken up next to. Walking to the window, he watched as the morning broke.

Then, turning, he walked back and sat in a chair close to the bed and watched Kay sleep. Thinking about the last couple of months and what had happened the night before, along with the fact it's been years since he's let anyone get close to him. Taking a deep breath, he again thought of his past, along with the fact that the Colombia cocaine cartels still have a price on him.

Deep in thought, he took a sip of coffee. *Can I protect her? Can we live in peace and not have to worry every day that my cover will be blown again?*

He sat and watched as the room got lighter. Glancing now and then at Kay.

Wow, she is beautiful and so damn sweet.

Standing up, he walked to the bed. Sitting down next to Kay, he slowly stroked her hair as he continued to sip his coffee and thought about his past and now their future.

Kay's eyes slowly opened as she inhaled the fantastic aroma of fresh coffee. Joe stooped to gently kiss her as he said, "Good morning, sunshine." He handed her the cup as she sat up in bed. Joe's eyes took in all of her womanly charm and beauty. He continued to look at the beautiful woman he had just woken up next to.

Slowly, Kay took her first sip as she said, "I could get really used to having you around. This is a fantastic way to wake up. Hot coffee being served in bed by a very sweet guy."

Joe knew he was in trouble. He had already fallen in love with her, although he was still scared to say it. Now he had to protect her and hopefully keep her away from his past.

Kay took another sip. Putting down her cup, she took his hand and said, "I think I love you." Pausing, she says, "No. I know I love you," as she met his eyes and then his lips.

Carefully, Joe kissed her. "I missed you every day I was

gone. I'm quite sure I love you, too. No, you are right. I *know* I have fallen in love with you."

Kay smiled and stood; she picked up her robe and said, "Hold that thought. I'll be right back." She headed for the bathroom.

Joe sat on the edge of the bed and as Kay returned. He handed her the coffee cup and said, "I knew you were someone special. I just wasn't expecting to fall in love with you and definitely not this quick."

Kay took a sip and said, "I think I fell in love with you when we met for coffee that first day. I just needed to wait and think about my feelings before I said anything."

Joe asked, "Do you have to work today?"

"No silly, it's Saturday."

"Wow, really." Pausing, he thought and then continued, "Let's go shopping and get a few groceries. Then spend the day relaxing right here. Say maybe watch a movie. Talk and I'll cook some ribs on that grill of yours. I have a great recipe."

Kay smiled. "Now, how can I turn that down. Have a good-looking guy cook for me."

"Okay. You cooked last night. Today, I'll make everything."

Kay smiled. "Even refill my cup?"

She handed it to him, and Joe reached for the cup. He grabbed his own, then headed for the kitchen. Filling both cups, he turned to see Kay standing just a few feet away. That black robe left very little to the imagination. Taking her in his arms, he gently kissed her and said, "Sit down and enjoy your coffee while I make you breakfast."

Kay smiled, sitting down. She sipped on her coffee; answering a few questions as Joe prepared pan-fried potatoes, eggs, bacon, and toast. Placing a plate in front of her, he pulled out a chair. While enjoying breakfast, they made plans for the day.

While shopping, Joe found two full racks of baby back ribs along with the barbecue sausage he liked and apple juice. Next, he needed a meat tenderizer and aluminum foil. Not used to shopping for more than a few days, he stared at the cart Kay was pushing. Putting his stuff in with hers, they headed for the checkout, then home.

While Kay put the groceries away, Joe walked out and started the grill. Setting the temperature for two hundred and turning on the smoke option. Double checking the pellet supply, he walked back in and started to prepare the ribs.

First, he removed most of the membrane on the back. Grabbing a sharp knife, he trimmed away the remaining membrane and squared off the ends.

Next, he rubbed the tenderizer on the meat side only on one rack. Taking out the aluminum foil, he made two bags he'll need later.

With the grill already hot, he made sure the heat shield was closed and placed the ribs directly grilling on both sides of the center. Setting the timer on his phone for two and a half hours, he walked back inside to help Kay.

With everything put away, Kay made another pot of coffee. With two cups and a craft, they head for the living room and pick a movie.

***

Just as the movie ended, Joe's alarm went off. Getting up, he headed for the kitchen. Taking the bottle of apple juice and the two bags he made earlier, he headed for the grill. With tongs, he put each rack in a bag and added a cup of apple juice, sealing the end. Placing them back on the grill, meat side down, he set the timer for two hours and headed back to the living room where Kay was waiting with two bottles of beer.

With another movie started, he sat next to Kay, who snuggled in under his arm, and they enjoyed another movie and chatted about different areas she would like to see.

"Have you ever been to Zion Park in Utah?"

Joe smiled and said, "Yes, several times. A couple of years ago, a zoo in Florida got permits for eight desert big horns. They hired me to find and live to trap them. It took about six weeks to find and catch eight sheep. They had permits for three rams and five ewes. Trying to find five ewes without kits was the problem. I had the three rams in just a few days, although the female was a problem. The state did not want ewes with kits to go. So, I looked for weeks before I finally had all five." About then, his alarm went off.

Joe headed back to the kitchen and, taking a stick of butter, he grabbed a saucepan and melted the butter. He mixed in a cup of brown sugar and one teaspoon of salt and a half cup of apple juice. Letting this simmer, he grabbed a small bowl and a bottle of KC barbecue sauce. With a brush and both sauces, he headed for the grill. Taking the ribs out of the bags, he put them back on the grill meat up and brushed on the sauces. One type on each. Setting the alarm for an hour, he went inside and grabbed two more beers before joining Kay in the dining room, where she was looking at a map of Montana. Looking at Joe, she asked, "Where's your cabin?"

Joe pointed at an area southwest of Missoula. "Right, about here. It's 40 miles south and west of Missoula, about 15 miles from Lolo Hot Springs."

"Will you take me there someday? Maybe someday soon."

Joe replied, "I would love to take you there. But why? Why would you want to go to a little cabin in the mountains? It's very primitive. I do have running water though. It's a hand pump in the kitchen sink. If you want to take a shower, you have to heat the water in a wood stove then fill the ten-gallon tank above the shower in the bathroom. There's an inside toilet now. I finished the inside plumbing this summer. I also put in electricity this summer. I'm hoping next summer to finish most of what's left."

Kay sat there with stars in her eyes, listening to him as he continued to talk about his little cabin. She asked, "How big is it? Oh, and how much land do you have?"

Joe smiled. "When I first started, it was just a three-room cabin with a kitchen, living room with one bedroom, and a bathroom. The whole thing was about twenty-five by forty. I've added on a few times, it's now about thirty-five hundred square feet. With four bedrooms, two full bathrooms, one half bath, a kitchen, and dining room plus the living room. I bought three hundred acres about eight years ago, and I've worked on it every summer. It's built completely out of logs off my land and so far, I've paid cash for everything."

Kay sat up and said, "Thirty-five hundred square foot cabin in the mountains on three hundred acres. My God, Joe, that's not a cabin. It's a mountain retreat. Do you have any idea on what it's worth?"

Joe replied, "Not really. The tax guy said it's still unfinished, and you can't live in most of it. So, my taxes are cheap, plus the fact that I've done all of this alone with no outside financial help. I designed everything as I went. There's a fireplace in every bedroom, plus one in the living room. I still have the old wood-burning stove in the kitchen that heats most of it. Until this summer, I had a big generator that supplied all the electricity I needed to build it. You can't get to it in the winter. Just too much snow. Plus, the fact that the driveway is just an old logging road that I rebuild every spring."

Glancing at his phone, he got up and headed for the grill.

Reappearing in the kitchen a few minutes later with supper, Kay quickly got up, grabbing plates and silverware. A few minutes later, Joe placed two half racks of ribs on Kay's plate, along with a baked potato and corn on the cob, all cooked on the grill.

Kay looked at her plate and said, "Wow that looks and smells absolutely fantastic."

"You have a two-half racks. Please try some of both. Then tell me which one you like better."

"They are both fantastic, although I think I like these a little better. Why? What's the difference?"

Joe smiled. "The one has a meat tenderizer on it along with KC's original barbecue sauce. The one you like has no tenderizer and my own recipe for the sauce."

Taking a few more bites, she said, "Use your own sauce from now on. I do like it better."

With supper done and the kitchen cleaned up, Joe went out and quickly cleaned the grill. Covering it up, he headed back inside to where Kay was sitting with two cups of tea and a movie ready to go. Sitting down, he picked up the tea and gave her a kiss as she pushed play.

***

Two hours later, Kay stood and headed for the bedroom. She walked back into the living room a few minutes later and said, "I'm thinking we should head for bed. I have to work tomorrow. You are staying tonight, aren't you?"

Joe looked at her standing there. Then he looked into her incredible eyes. "I'd be a fool to leave such a beautiful woman and such an inviting invitation. Besides, I haven't been compared to God yet today."

Kay laughed, taking both of his hands. "I know I love you, and I don't just love you, but I'm *in* love with you. There is a difference, you know."

As Joe pulled her a little closer, bending forward, he kissed her lightly. "I think I fell in love with you that night we met. I know I did the following day while drinking coffee." Then, taking her into his arms, he bent forward again and kissed her gently on the forehead, then the lips, and together, they walked down the hall to their waiting bedroom.

Joe woke the following morning and slid quietly out of bed. Slipping sweatpants on, he headed for the kitchen. Fixing coffee, he was sitting at the kitchen table when he heard the shower start and a few minutes later, stopped. Getting up, he poured another cup and placed it on the nightstand on Kay's side of the bed. Going back to the kitchen, he made breakfast. He was just flipping the eggs when Kay walked into the kitchen, all ready for work. Pouring another cup, she said, "Oh my God. First, coffee waiting for me in the bedroom, now breakfast ready and waiting on the table. I'm going to get really spoiled."

Kay reached and grabbed her purse, saying, "What are your plans for the day?" Handing him a key, she continued,

"Here's a key to the house. I should be home early."

Taking the key, he says, "I'm going to go check on the plane and get it ready. You want to see my cabin? We can go anytime you can get away for a couple of days."

"Are you serious? I have months of vacation time coming. When do you what to go?"

"We can leave tomorrow morning if you want to. You decide when you can get away. I'm free until September unless someone calls."

Kay smiled. "I'll check with my boss and see when I can take a week off. Is that enough time? I can ask for more?"

Joe filled both coffee cups. "A week would be great. We can do a little sightseeing and maybe even work on it some."

Kay snickered. "I'm not much of a carpenter. Although I learn quickly, and I can always just watch you."

"Okay, I'll get the plane ready, and you see when you can go. Call me as soon as you know anything." He kissed her, and Kay took her last swallow. Getting up, she headed toward the garage. Joe followed her out. Opening the car door, he kissed her one more time before she headed for work. Watching until she was out of sight, he went in and cleaned up, locked the door, and headed for the airport.

Walking around the plane a couple of times, he climbed in and started the engines. Taxiing across the tarmac, he stopped by the fuel pumps and shut down. Getting out, he grabbed the gas nozzle and fueled the plane just as the airport fuel jockey walked up. Joe topped off all four tanks and was inside paying when his phone beeped. Looking at the screen, he saw it was Kay. Pushing the button, he said, "Hello, sunshine."

"I can go tomorrow and be gone a week or more. All I have to do is let him know. Do you have cell service by your cabin?"

"My phone does. So hopefully yours will, too. If not, you can use mine for an additional charge. Say a couple of kisses."

"I'll be home in a couple of hours. We can get packed and leave in the morning."

Joe taxied the plane back to the hangar. Putting it inside, he spent the next couple of hours going over it and cleaning it up. Looking at his watch, he headed for Kay's.

Walking into the house, he saw two suitcases in the kitchen and Kay coming from the bedroom with a garment bag and another smaller case. Joe said, "Whoa, slow down. It's a Cessna 310, not a 747, there are a few things I need to bring, so we have to pack light."

Kay looked at him and says, "I did pack light."

Joe started to laugh. "Honey, let's go through what you've packed and figure out just what we have to bring." Picking up the two suitcases, he said, "Come on, sweetie, follow me."

After going through what she had packed, Joe carried one suitcase and her makeup bag to the pickup, throwing his duffel on top. They were ready for an early morning departure.

After supper, with everything cleaned up, they settled down to watch a little television with a cup of tea. Kay asked, "What do you want to try and get done?"

"Not much. Maybe just a little plumbing. I really just want you to see it and the area around. We'll fly over and around it a few times before landing. I have a Jeep at the airport, and we'll use it to get up there. There are a few logging or forestry roads. Although we can hike almost anywhere you want to go. I'm sure we'll do a little of both."

Chapter Seven

At 5:00 a.m., Joe woke up and showered. Heading for the kitchen, he made a coffee. Pouring two cups, he carried one, and put it down next to Kay on the nightstand. Then he headed back to the kitchen.

A few minutes later, a sleepy Kay walked in, saying, "Good morning. My God, the birds aren't even up yet."

Joe smiled. Getting up, he filled her cup again and said, "Drink that and take a shower. It's a long flight out there, and I'm sure we'll be landing several times along the way. I've already got a flight plan filed and a route figured out. We are going to fly VFR, or visual flight rules, although I filed it IFR, or instrument flight rules. There are a few places we might hit some weather. If it's not a thunderstorm, I'll fly through. Thunderstorms, we go around. Most of the route looks to be clear, and I want to be on the ground in Lolo before dark. I can get vectored in, but there are rocks in the sky around there. That makes after dark flying a little dangerous."

Kay had a puzzled look on her face and said, "Rocks in the sky?"

Joe laughed. "Oops. I should have said mountains."

Kay smiled. "Yes, okay, now that makes sense. You're right, I don't want to run into one of them."

An hour later, with Kay now awake, Joe loaded everything

onto the plane. Putting the heaviest into the nose compartment. Then filling it with whatever he could fit. The lightest things went in the back seat, with the heaviest right behind the front seats. With the plane loaded, Joe pulled it out of the hangar and looked at the way it's setting. Looking one more time at the weight and balance chart, he saw it was inside the envelope. Double checking his math with full tanks, he said, "I think we can go. Everything checks out." Then, smiling, he added, "If you told me your correct weight."

Still laughing, he helped Kay up the wing, showing her where to put her feet, and said, "Please don't step out any farther than that red line." Then, going around, he checked the control surfaces one more time before getting in and doing a pre-startup check. With both engines running, he taxied to the active runway, waiting for takeoff instructions and clearance.

With clearance granted, he pushed the throttles and props forward, gaining speed. With the plane wheels up, they turn to the west, headed for a week of fun and togetherness.

Joe keyed the mike and opened the flight plan. Then, flipping a couple of switches, he said, "These new radios Bluetooth to my phone. I have a music mix on there. Want to listen to it?"

"Absolutely, that would be great. Wow, you can see a long way. How far off the ground are we?"

Glancing at the altimeter, he replied, "Eight thousand five hundred feet."

Kay looked around, then straight down. "It looks like we are hardly moving. How fast are we going?"

Glancing at the instruments, he said, "Our air speed is 210 miles per hour. Although we have a tail wind, and our ground speed is just short of 250 miles per hour."

Kay looked back at the ground. "Wow, really? You sure can't tell it."

"It's the altitude. It plays tricks on your eyes. We are already over Wisconsin and will be over Minnesota in about an hour. It's just over a thousand miles, and if the wind stays with us, we'll be there in about four hours, maybe just a shade more. Oh, there's a volume knob on the right side of your headset. You can turn it up or down." Pausing for a minute, he continued, "If we start to talk or if a voice comes over the radio, it'll automatically turn off the music. If you push that button on the yoke, you can talk with air traffic control or other airplanes." He reached across and shows her. "Now, the other is for trimming the plane for level flight, climbing or descent."

***

Joe landed at a small airport in southern Minnesota. He was sure Kay's bladder was full by now. The telltale sign, by the way she was wiggling around. It was usually a very good sign. He shut down the passenger's side engine while on the taxiway, knowing Kay would want out as soon as the plane stopped. Joe taxied up to the pumps, and as soon as the plane stopped, Kay was out and running for the terminal and restroom. Joe finished shutting down the plane, telling the fuel attendant, "Top off both tip tanks. I haven't drawn off the main tanks yet." With that, he walked inside to find a smiling Kay standing by the counter and saying, "I made it."

Joe laughed. "That's good. From now on, tell me when you first feel the need to go. I can usually find an airport in a few minutes. I noticed how you were wiggling around, or we would still be en-route. I'll be right back." He headed for the men's restroom.

Coming out a few minutes later, he took her by the hand, and they walked into the pilot's briefing room. Looking at the weather radar and forecast, he said, "Looks like clear skies and mostly smooth air well into Montana." Printing off a copy of the forecast, they paid for the gas, and a few minutes later, Joe pushed the throttles forward again as the Cessna lifts skyward, and they once again head west.

After landing three more times, once in North Dakota and twice in Montana, Kay nearly jumped out of her skin when Joe reached over and nudged her awake, saying, "Is something wrong? What's going on?"

Joe smiled as he continued to pull the power back. Lifting his hand, he pointed out Kay's side window and says, "There it is."

Kay tried to answer but ended up saying, "Are we ... umm ... is that? Is everything? Where are we?"

Joe snickered. "We are in western Montana. You've been asleep since before we crossed the divide. That's my cabin below us and slightly behind now. Give me a minute. I'll turn around and make another pass. Then we'll land and go up there."

Pushing the power full, he pulled the plane into a steep climb and started making the turn. Half-way around, he pulled the power again and dropped the nose as they passed over it in a steep bank. Leveling off, he headed for the airport in Lolo, Montana.

With the plane tied down, Joe again found Kay standing by the counter. Giving her a quick kiss, he said, "I'll be right back. Meet me by the plane. We can get everything loaded into the Jeep, and you'll be eating food cooked on an old cast iron wood-burning stove. Probably one very similar to what your grandma cooked on in about two hours."

With everything loaded, Joe stopped at a local supermarket and grab just enough food for their supper.

As they headed towards the cabin, Kay asked, "Why didn't you get more?"

"There's electricity up there now. The way I have it wired; the generator should come on if the power goes out. I also have a pantry full of supplies. As long as an animal like a bear has not broken in."

He stopped at the turn onto the logging road that went to his cabin. He opened his duffel and grabbed a .44 magnum

Ruger Redhawk and a box of shells. Checking the loops are all full, he slipped six into the cylinder and flipped it closed. Strapping it on, he checked a second one. Handing it to Kay, he said, "I'm sure we won't need these, although it's better to have them and not need them than to need it and not have them. That's a .357. If we need it, use both hands. It has a bit of a jump to it."

Kay smiled. "Yes, I know, I've shot one several times. I like my 9mm much better."

Joe turned and looked at her. "Are you ready?"

Kay nodded her head as Joe put the Jeep back in gear, and they started up the logging road that'll take them to his mountain hideaway.

Rounding the last corner, the cabin came into sight. Kay's mouth dropped open as she saw it. Parking in front, Joe said, "Stay here, let me get things opened, checked out, and turned on."

A few minutes later, he walked back and said, "All open, let's get settled in."

Kay grabbed a suitcase and followed Joe inside, where she walked around in a state of shock. The place was amazing, with hand-drawn logs. A huge split rock fireplace and an old wood-burning cast iron cook stove. Joe took her to their bedroom. She walked into the huge bathroom with a clawfoot cast iron bathtub, a huge two-headed shower plus a washer and dryer in the master bath. Grabbing a flashlight, he led Kay through the rest of the house, saying, "I built this as my retirement home. I got a little carried away in some areas, although if I should ever decide to sell, it should bring a good price."

Kay walked toward the front of the house and stood there mesmerized. A beautiful mountain valley spread out in front of her. Turning, she said, "That view alone is worth a million dollars."

Joe walked up and said, "Yeah, I stand up here and look at that every morning while drinking my coffee. I don't think I'll ever get tired of it."

"Why didn't you put your bedroom up here?"

"This was the first add on and I already have a bedroom built. Follow me. Let me show you something."

Walking back down the stairs, Joe walked outside and opened the shutters on the bedroom windows. Then, back inside, he opened the drapes. Kay stood there staring at another million-dollar view and said, "Oh my God. Does every room have that kind of view?"

"All the bedrooms do, although the kitchen just looks out over the driveway. I didn't want to change where it was."

"Can we eat up here tonight?"

Joe smiled. "Nope, follow me." He went up another set of stairs to a rooftop deck. Pointing to the west, he said, "Let's eat here where we can watch the sunset."

Kay wrapped her arms around him. "Any more

surprises?"

"Only one. We do have running water in the lower part of the house, along with a flushing toilet. I checked when I opened everything up. The well and septic are done, and everything is hooked up. That's about the only thing I didn't do myself. I've already filled and turned on the water heater. Let's go start supper. I'm thinking the steaks we bought along with pan-fried potatoes."

Getting to the kitchen, Joe built a fire in the old cast iron cook stove. Next, he grabbed the steaks and a medium-size cast iron frying pan. Putting the frying pan on the stove, he dropped in a stick of butter. Reaching for the potatoes, he sliced them up along with a small onion and green peppers. Next, he pushed everything into the pan. Then, he grabbed a huge cast iron pan. Putting it on the stove, he dropped in butter and garlic. While that was warming up, he took the two steaks and dusted a fair amount of prime rib rub; he put the first one in the pan. Covering both pans, he grabbed two bottles of beer. Handing one to Kay, he said, "I'm going to see what we have in the pantry for a vegetable. Plus, look in that bag. I think they put the wine in there."

Kay took the wine and followed Joe into the walk-in pantry. Seeing a refrigerator just inside the door, she put it in the freezer, saying, "It should be cold by the time we are ready to eat."

Canned goods were stacked on shelves on both sides.

Getting to the end, she saw two large chest type freezers. Pointing at the freezers then looking at Joe, she asks, "Why in here and why two?"

"I usually get one elk plus a deer every year. I always apply for a moose and sheep tag. If I happened to draw all of them, I would need room. I put them in here to put extra doors between all my supplies and the outside. A bear would make the biggest mess you have ever seen. This helps to ensure that won't happen. Like the heavy shutters I have on all the ground-level windows. Plus, when I close this up for the winter, I nail four by eight sheets of plywood over all the doors. It's just extra security but it's been working. I've never had an animal get inside, plus I've never had anyone break-in."

Walking back to the kitchen, Joe flipped the steak and put in the other. Next, he dropped in a full can of mushrooms. Grabbing a container marked sea salt, he salted the mushroom and stirred in the remaining onions. Opening a can of corn into a third pan, he placed it on the stove. Fifteen minutes later, they walked up the stairs and sat at a table on the rooftop deck to enjoy a fantastic meal while watching the sunset over the Rocky Mountains.

Kay lifted her wine glass. "Great meal cooked by a fantastic guy and in the most beautiful scenery I think I've ever seen."

Joe lifted his glass and touched hers. Taking a sip, he

reached over, gave her a soft kiss, and said, "With fantastic company."

With supper dishes all cleaned up, Joe filled the fire box again and choked the fire down as low as he could. Opening their bedroom door, he then grabbed two more beers, and they headed upstairs to enjoy an evening under the stars.

Morning broke in the mountains cool and clear as Joe rolled out of bed to fix coffee. Coals were still dancing in the firebox's bottom with a few smaller pieces, then some bigger ones. In a few minutes, the old stove took the morning chill off, replacing it with the smell of a wood fire. With the coffee on, Joe headed for the shower.

Coming out a few minutes later, he jumped as Kay said, "Really great coffee this morning." Pausing, she continued, "I'm sorry, I didn't mean to startle you. Do you always wake up before the birds?"

Joe snickered. "I'm not used to having anyone else around, although I love having you here. I wasn't expecting you to be up yet. And yes, I've always been an early riser." Taking the offered cup, he said, "Give the water heater a few minutes and you can get a shower while I make breakfast."

They spent the first morning cutting lodge pole pine that would be used at a later time. Then, they finished the railing on the three sets of stairs. Joe worked on the plumbing in the upstairs bathroom until he ran out of parts. Making a list of what else he would need, they quit for the day to spend some time together.

That evening, they had supper on the rooftop deck again. With the plumbing finished to the master bath, Joe opened the valves and checked for leaks. He had plumbed the place so he could turn off the water to about any room in the house while still having water in the rest of the house. He showed Kay where the valves were, just in case. After supper, they moved from the downstairs bedroom to the master suite on the main floor. Kay absolutely loved the view, and Joe simply loved Kay.

The following morning, after breakfast, they made a picnic lunch and headed for the mountains. As always, Joe grabbed his pistol and handed the other to Kay, saying, "Here, put this on. I've already checked, and it's ready to go."

Belting on the two handguns, they got into an old military Jeep and started up the mountain. There was a spot Joe wanted to show her. About ten miles back into the mountains, they rounded a corner and Joe stopped. In front of them was an incredible sight. A waterfall and the stream were running full. The rain they had gotten in the last couple of days had brought it to nearly flood stage. All Kay could do was sit and stare. Joe sat there looking at her as she looked at the water plummeting nearly fifty feet into a swollen pool and the fast-moving rapids below them. Getting out, Joe took her hand, and they carefully traversed the steep rock-filled mountain side to the pool's edge.

Looking at Joe, Kay asked, "Every time I think I just saw the most beautiful place ever, you show me something better." Gazing around in scenery shock, all she could do was point. Then, turning back, she asked, "Is that deep? Can I go in?"

"It's very deep. That waterfall has had a couple of million years to excavate a deep hole in the rock. The sides are steep and really slippery. A slip and fall could mean one of us is carrying the other out."

Kay continued to look around as he led her back to the old Jeep. Putting the Jeep in gear, he said, "I think we'll keep going for now. We can come back here in an hour or two."

Kay would point at one place, then another. Joe just sat there, smiling. She was having a blast, and he was enjoying every second. The scenery was nothing short of magnificent. Topping the mountain, Joe stopped again as the valley below came into full sight. Kay slowly got out of the Jeep and walked to the edge. Looking some eight hundred feet straight down. Stepping back, she asked, "How far is it across to the other side of the valley?"

"From here, it's probably thirty miles, maybe more."

Joe walked up, putting his arms around her as she stood mesmerized by the scenery. Joe said, "Let's see how good of a shot you are. I've got a target with me." Walking back, Joe grabbed the target and stepped off about thirty feet. Walking back, he handed earplugs to Kay, then the .357. Kay took the gun, aimed and fired. Joe watched, adjusted her grip and stance, and she shot a few more. Putting the gun down, they walked to the target. Her first two were low and right. The last four were high and center. Joe showed her why the first two were low and right, saying, "A right-handed person almost always pulls the gun right as they pull the trigger. The way I change your grip helped you remain on target."

Kay was looking at Joe when her eyes grew, and just as she started to say something, Joe placed his hand over her mouth and said, "Stay behind me and do as I tell you when I tell you. Do you have your pistol?"

Joe's eyes never left the huge grizzly bear standing just past the Jeep. Kay whispered, "No, it's next to yours on the seat."

"Okay, follow me but stay back about three feet. If it charges, stand your ground." Glancing around quickly, he continued, "See those rocks over there to the right about twenty feet?"

Kay glanced. "Yes, that big pile?"

"Yes. If I say, run. Get to those rocks and climb like your life depends on it. Because it does."

Joe slowly bent and picked up a branch he could use as a club if needed. Then slowly, walked toward the Jeep. Slowly, step by step, they closed the distance. With just five feet left, the bear started to walk around the rear of the Jeep. Joe changed directions and headed for the front. With the bear behind and them in front, they have momentary safety.

As the bear started to come around, Joe grabbed Kay and swung her past him. He grabbed his hand cannon and touched the trigger, firing a warning shot into the ground. The bear growled and woofed several times as Joe stood with it in his sights. Slowly, the huge old bruin turned and slowly walked off.

Kay let out her breath she didn't know she had been holding and started to shake. She then slid down the side of the Jeep to the ground. Joe placed the pistol on the hood and picked her up. Walking around the Jeep, he carefully put her down in the passenger seat. Grabbing his belt and holster, he strapped it on. Then, picking up the pistol, he opened the cylinder and replaced the spent cartridge with a loaded one. Sliding it back into the holster, he looked at where the bear had disappeared into the woods, saying, "I'm sure he's gone, although I'm going to walk over and check to make sure."

Kay grabbed his arm. "No, you're not. You stay right here by me. In fact, let's go somewhere else. I don't want to see him again today and hopefully never again."

Joe reached down, putting his arms around her. "A gun shot to those guys usually means food. He saw us, but he didn't smell blood. He just wanted to make sure."

"Are we on the or in the food chain with him?"

Joe replied, "Not as a general rule. Grizzlies do attack and kill people, although it's usually caused by people doing something stupid. Like leaving food lying around."

"Do they eat us?"

Joe looked straight into her eyes and said, "Yes, they have been known to kill and eat people. When we are together and something like this happens, listen to me and do exactly what I say. Ninety-nine times out of a hundred, everything will end in our favor. I've run into bears several times. And I've never had to kill one."

Kay smiled, stepping out of the Jeep; she wrapped her arms around him. "You are a remarkable man. I have never felt this safe around anyone."

Joe hugged her tight. "I'll always protect you out here or in the city. That, I promise."

***

The following morning, after coffee and breakfast, Joe got out a heavy barrel .308. He stood there as a rush of memories came over him. The gun felt so familiar. He has shot this rifle hundreds, if not thousands, of times. Opening the action and putting down the bipod, he walked over and put a target up. Then he placed several rocks and branches on a log. Looking at Kay, he asked, "How do you do with a rifle?"

"I've shot one a few times. I used to hunt some."

Joe smiled and said, "Okay, let's try by dry firing. Just get a feel for the trigger. Try to remember when it's going to go off. After a few dry firings, he said, "Let's start with the target.

Kay slid the action shut and pulled the trigger. High and

right. Joe said, "One more." She worked the bolt and pulled the trigger. High and right again. He made an adjustment to the scope and said, "Again, two more." Kay lined up and pulled the trigger. High but center. Joe said, "Pick a target on the log. Kay put the crosshairs on a rock, pulled the trigger and missed. Joe said, "Try squeezing it a little slower. You're pulling too fast. Slow down and try again."

Kay placed the crosshairs again and slowly squeezed the trigger. The rock jumped straight up and back out of sight. She continued to shoot as Joe gave her advice and in an hour; she was hitting every time.

Kay looked at Joe. "How good of a shot are you?"

"I'm sure I could hit the side of that mountain over there. If it holds still."

"No, really. I would like to see."

Joe picked up the rifle and let its balance work into his muscle memory for a few seconds, then said, "See that branch on that tree over there? On the dead pine?"

Kay replied, "What dead pine?"

Joe put the gun down and grabbed a spotting scope. Zeroing in on the branch, he told Kay the one in the middle of that scope. Kay looked through the scope, then over the top and back to the scope. The number at the bottom of the scope said four hundred sixty-two yards. She looked at Joe and said, "You're kidding, right?"

Joe smiled. "Nope." Making a few adjustments, he slowly

squeezed the trigger, and the branch disappeared.

Kay turned and looked at him, saying, "Oh my God. You just hit that at over four hundred yards."

Smiling, Joe replied, "Yeah, I've made shots farther than that."

Kay took the scope and looked around. Seeing a white rock on the mountainside, she said, "See that white rock over there on the side of the mountain?"

Joe looked through the scope and said, "Yes, it's just under six hundred yards."

Kay looked through the scope and asked, "How did you do that?"

Joe showed her a button. "Just push that button. It's a laser ranger finder and spotting scope."

Kay asks, "Can you hit that?"

Joe zeroed the scope. Making an adjustment, he slowly squeezed the trigger. A puff of white dust sprayed into the air as the 125 grain Sierra bonded boat tail bullet found its mark and the rock rolled down the hill out of sight.

Kay turned. "Where did you learn to shoot like that?"

"I've hunted since I was old enough to carry a gun. Then I spent four years in the military. I guess they fine-tuned my shooting skills. Let's go inside and have something quick to eat and start closing this place up. We can stay in a motel in town tonight and head for Chicago tomorrow."

Joe walked inside, going through the house, making sure

every window was closed and locked. Double checking the dampeners in the fireplaces, he walked back to the lower floor, shutting off the power to the entire house, except for the pantry where an electric heater kept the small room about fifty degrees and also powered the two freezers and refrigerator. Next, he opened all the drains and water started flowing backwards out of the pipes. He then opened the water heater. Double checking that the dampeners in the cook stove were closed, he walked outside.

Making sure all the shutters were closed and locked together, they walked around the house double checking, making sure everything was closed, locked, and put away.

Throwing everything in the old Jeep, they started the long, slow drive off the mountain and headed for town. Checking into a motel, Joe said, "Let's go to the airport and load most of our stuff tonight. We only need one small case and your makeup."

With the plane loaded, they headed back to the motel and supper at the restaurant. After supper, they walked a couple of blocks to a small bar. Enjoying a beer, they talked about what they had gotten done and what was left to do next summer. Looking at her watch, Kay gave Joe a very seductive look and smile. "I'm tired. It's been a long day. What do you think about going back to the room and calling it an early night?"

Joe smiled as he stood and pulled Kay's chair out, saying,

"That sounds like a fantastic idea. I could use a little extra sleep."

Kay reached up and whispered, "You are not going to get very much extra sleep." Winking at him, she walked away toward the restroom.

Joe smiled as he watched her walk away. He paid their tab and waited for her to return. Walking back to the motel, Kay reached over and took his hand. Joe pulled her a little closer and put his arm around her as they walked in silence for the last block. Arriving back at their room, Joe reached over and unlocked the door. Easing Kay through, he put the *Do Not Disturb* sign into the knob and closed and locked the door.

***

Joe's eyes snapped open. Something wasn't right. Some slight unusual noise woke him. Lying perfectly still, he listened. Moving only his eyes, he saw the light in the room change. He made a fist under the covers as he felt the bed move. Pivoting nearly in place, he grabbed Kay and pulled her down just as he recognized her and kissed her. Kay was about to scream when she felt his lips on hers. Kissing her romantically, he said, "Is it my turn for the shower?"

Kay replied, "You scared the crap out of me. I thought you were sleeping, and I didn't want to wake you."

"I think I was but I heard the door open so I figured I would surprise you."

"Well, you surprised me okay and scared me out of ten

years."

"I'll give you back the ten years and the rest of my life to go with them." Getting up, he headed for the shower.

Closing the door, he looked at himself in the mirror and thought, *Well, Randy, you could have really hurt her. You have to learn how to be with someone and you had better learn fast. You're Joe now. Forget Randy and that life. It's all behind you.*

With the shower over, Joe opened the door wrapped in a towel and wearing his t-shirt. Shutting off the lights, he dropped the towel, removed his shirt and slipped into bed next to a very warm and receptive Kay.

***

Joe's eyes flickered a few times before opening. It was just before sunrise. Slipping out of bed, he pulled a shirt over his head and put on a pair of sweats. Slipping on his shoes, he headed toward the office and took a coffee pot. Grabbing a craft, he filled it and picked up two cups. Opening the door to the room, Kay was just getting out of bed. Joe looked at her as he poured the coffee. Kay finished belting her robe as they walked out onto the balcony. They watched as the eastern sky turned a shade of purple, then blue. Joe filled Kay's cup again and said, "I'm going to take a quick shower. I'll be back here in a few minutes." He bent down and kissed her tenderly and walked back into the room.

Kay laid back and put her feet up. Totally relaxed and thinking about the night before. In just a few short days, Joe had learned her body and knew what she wanted and needed. She was in love. Of that, there was no doubt.

Joe walked back onto the balcony and looked at Kay. She was sound asleep again. Carefully, he sat down and poured another cup. Going over everything they had done, plus thinking about closing it up for the winter. He was going over a mental checklist as Kay started to move and woke up.

Joe asked, "Do you remember locking the door going to the rooftop deck?"

Kay sat there thinking. "No, I don't think I did. Did you?"

"No, I don't. I think I'm going to run back up there and check. Why don't you relax a little longer and enjoy the sunrise? Drink a few more cups and I should be back in a few hours. Maybe take a bath with that new book you brought with you. What is it called again?"

Kay got up and walked to her small suitcase. Opening it, she picked up the book and said, "Deadly Desire. It's his second in this series, and I can't find the first. Every time I check online it says sold out. I know I'll get it sooner or later. It's just that I want them all. I looked just before we left and there's an ad for the next two. Surviving Evil and Justifiable Vengeance. I can't wait to get them."

Joe got up and filled her cup. Bending down, he kissed her deeply, smiled and headed for the cabin. Kay set back and opened the book, reading.

***

Logan sat astride his beautiful paint stallion on the top of the bluff that overlooked a river valley that ran through the northern part of his 75,000-acre ranch.

Joe reached the house and started to walk around so he could climb to the rooftop deck. Coming around a corner, he saw two guys looking at the house. Joe reached for the pistol that wasn't there. Walking up to them, he said, "Can I help you?"

The two men jumped as they heard his voice. Walking to Joe, they said in broken English, "We are looking for a guy named Randy Jackson."

Joe never missed a beat. Standing there with a thoughtful look on his face, he said, "Randy Jackson. I don't think I know the name. Although, I'm still building this as you can see and I'm only here a few months in the summer. Say, have you checked in town. Maybe someone there can help you."

One guy turned toward Joe and then his partner and said, "Hey Diego, that's a great idea."

Diego turned and replied, "Yeah Diaz, why didn't you think of that?"

Joe looked and saw teardrop tattoos on both of their cheeks, thinking, *Great, these two dickheads are MS-13. That's a gang from Colombia, or at least that area.*

Walking back toward the driveway, Joe put out his hand and said, "I'm Joe West."

Diego took the offered hand and pulled a knife. Joe

unleashed a powerful left that connected with his chin. Diego's eyes rolled up, and he dropped to the ground.

Spinning, he watched as Diaz grabbed a pitchfork they had left outside. Looking around, Joe saw a broken garden rake handle.

Grabbing it, he turned to face Diaz, who was lunging forward. Joe blocked the lunge and, spinning around, he hooked the end of the chunk of his staff under Diaz's chin. Snapping his head back. Dropping down, he hooked his legs and pulled. Diaz hit the ground on his back. Joe swung the stick like a bat coming down on his stomach.

Looking around, he saw Diego trying to get to his feet. Joe stepped in and swung his staff like a baseball bat. Diego got his arm in the air to block the strike and heard a loud snap as Joe's swing broke his arm. Pivoting, he swung the other way and connected with the side of Diego's head with a sickening thump. Diego's eyes rolled up, and once again, he dropped.

Joe started to turn as Diaz lunged again, this time sticking the fork into his back. Joe let out a moan and jumped forward as he pushed from behind. He kept moving and felt the tines slide out as he did.

Swinging around quickly, he caught the other attacker off guard and swung the club again, connecting with the side of Diaz's head. It made a sound like a hammer hitting a pumpkin. Diaz screamed and dropped the fork as he grabbed his head. Joe drove the staff into his stomach, just below his ribs and up. Diaz made a gurgling sound and dropped to the ground. Looking at Diego, he walked over and drove the end of the rake handle into the same spot.

Stopping, he walked a few steps and sat down, breathing deeply and trying to think. *What the hell am I going to do now? Two dead MS-13 idiots in my driveway.* Reaching for his phone, he looked for a number. Pushing call, he listened, "The number you have dialed is not in service. Please check the number and try again. If you need help, call the operator."

Joe swore out loud as he searched for another number. Pushing call, he tried to collect himself as the phone rang. The receptionist answered, saying, "DEA can I help you?"

Joe said, "Adrian please."

The receptionist said, "I'm sorry, Adrian is no longer with us. He retired about six months ago."

"Do you have a phone number for him. This is Randy Jackson." Not wanting to give out his current name.

"I'm sorry sir, but we are not allowed to give that information out."

"Can you get a message to him and ask him to call me?"

"Yes sir, I'll try. Is there anything else I can do for you?"

Joe answered, "No ma'am, just that. I really need to talk to him."

"Okay, I'll see what I can do. Anything else?"

"Nope, just that. Please, I need to talk with him."

The receptionist hung up, threw the piece of paper away, and went back to work.

Joe sat there, thinking. Looking through his contacts, he saw the number for Judge Wallace. Pushing call, he waited as another receptionist answered, "Federal Court House, can I help you?"

Joe replied, "Yes, can I talk to Judge Wallace, please?"

"Oh, I'm sorry. Judge Wallace is no longer with us."

"Shit, is there a number I can get? Or can you get a message to him?"

"Sir, I'm so sorry but he was murdered about eight months ago."

Joe looked at his phone and pushed the end button. Taking a deep breath, he thought for a few minutes, *Oh, boy. I have two dead guys lying here. The judge that set up my new identity is dead, and Adrian has retired. I'm screwed.*

Walking over, he picked up both and threw them into the back of the Jeep. Next, he walked into the shed and got two of his older climbing harnesses, along with a few climbing tools like cam locks, climbing hammer and rope, and rock spikes. Then, he headed for the high country behind his house thinking, *Bears, wolves, coyotes. There are enough scavengers around here, they'll both be gone in a few weeks.*

Getting to the top of the mountain, he picked up one and walked to the cliff's edge. Putting on the climbing harness, he attached five cam locks and a couple of rock spikes. Next, he carried the other guy over and put the second harness on him. Connecting the rope, he pushed him over the ledge. He watched as the rope went taut and the second guy followed.

Getting back to the house, he climbed onto the roof and went inside. Getting to the master bath, he opened the bottom drawer and took out a first aid kit. Pausing, he just looked for a couple of minutes. Taking the first of several syringes, he removed the cap and stuck the needle into his leg. The antibiotic should keep him from getting sepsis. Removing his blood covered t-shirt, he filled the holes with a quick clot. Then, picking up a syringe with medical grade superglue, he pushed the needle inside the holes and pushed the plunger. Pushing about a fourth into the first hole. With his teeth clenched, he repeated the process again and again. Putting his bloody shirt, jeans, and jacket into a bag, he then cleaned up the best he can, got clean clothes and a jacket. Getting dressed, he headed for town, the motel, and Kay.

Dropping the bag into the motel dumpster, he walked inside and directly to their room and to a waiting Kay who asked, "What took you so long? Was the door open? I was scared you ran into that bear. Why didn't you call me? Are you going to answer me?"

Joe smiled as he replied, "I had a flat and didn't realize it took this long. Sorry." He reached over, pulling her close and kissed her. Then, picking up her bags, he said, "I'll be back in a minute." Walking out and to the Jeep, he slipped out his knife and pushed the blade into the face of the spare. Looking around, he put the knife away as he walked back to get Kay. Together, they walked hand in hand to the front desk to check out, then to the Jeep.

With the plane already fueled and loaded, Joe quickly threw in the last couple of bags while Kay was getting strapped in. He walked around doing his preflight. With everything checked out, he got in and started engine one, then two. Putting on the seat belts, he taxied to the active runway. Checking with local traffic, he lined up with the centerline. Pushing the props to takeoff, he eased the throttles forward and felt the Cessna gain speed and lift into the air. Reaching over, he gave Kay a quick kiss as he opened the flight plan. Flipping a couple of switches, the music came across the headset to help settle Kay down.

With everything set for flight, Joe flipped the switch to turn on the autopilot, relaxing, he started to think. *Are those two guys really MS-13 or just a couple of idiots. I had proved a connection between MS-13 and the cocaine cartels when I was in Colombia.*

Kay asked, "Can we land somewhere soon? I have to go to the bathroom."

Joe was deep in thought. "What? Umm, honey, what did you say? Sorry I missed that. I was, umm, looking at the radar," he lied.

"Joe, what's wrong with you? I asked twice. I need to go

to the bathroom."

Joe quickly looked at the flight GPS and said, "Yes, Livingston is just a few minutes ahead."

Talking to flight control, he closed the fight plan and pulled the power as he started losing altitude. Then set the plane up to land.

Shutting down the passenger side engine, he taxied to the terminal and shut the plane down completely. Walking inside, he showed Kay the restroom as he walked into the men's restroom. Waiting for Kay, he checked the weather again. As Kay came out, he asks, "Do you want anything before we get airborne again?"

Laughing, Kay replied, "No, I pee enough without adding more fluid."

With everything ready, in a few minutes, they were airborne and climbing. With the music playing, he started to think again, *Has my cover been blown again. I saw the tear drops they had tattooed on their cheeks. If they are MS-13, both are killers, or were they both imposters? Let's see, the judge is dead. Murdered from what I was told, and Adrian has retired. Am I on my own?*

I can call Colton, although what would he know? I think I had better just keep my eyes open and mouth shut. I can do this. I can protect her and myself.

He looked at Kay, who was now sleeping. Tears started slipping down his cheek. He loved her and there was nothing he could do about that. He knows he can't leave her, although that is what he should do. He can protect her. With that thought, he makes a silent promise to himself, *I will do what I need to do.*

Kay started to wake as Joe started pulling the power back.

Yawning and stretching, she asks, "Where are we?"

Joe answered as he turned base to final, "Steele ND. This time, I have to go."

Kay sat up, looking around, and said, "Wow, how long have I been sleeping?"

"Just a shade over three hours," he said as the nose came up and the plane floated in ground effect until it touched down.

Pulling up to the pumps, he shut down both engines. Stepping onto the wing, he told the fuel attendant, "Fill both main tanks."

They walked to the main terminal to find the restrooms.

Joe said, "I'll meet you in the pilot's room." He pointed down the hall.

With the tanks full and back in the air, in a few hours, Joe radioed air traffic control inbound Midway for land institutions. Then, he closed their flight plan, fueling the plane again, and they headed for the hanger.

Chapter Eight

Arriving back at Kay's house, they hauled their luggage into the house where Kay started putting things away and Joe started supper. As they finished cleaning up, Kay put on the water for tea and they headed for the living room and a cozy fire.

With first light, Joe got up, made coffee, and headed for the shower. All dressed and ready for the day, he poured a cup for Kay as she walked out of the shower and headed for the bedroom to finish dressing.

Sitting at the table, Kay said, "What are your plans for the day?"

"Well, I have a few calls to make. Plus, I think I had better check on an apartment for the winter. I'm staying in this area for at least the winter. Plus, the fact I can't freeload on you forever."

Kay slowly turned towards Joe and, with tears starting to form in her eyes, she asked, "Why do you need an apartment? What's wrong with staying here? Oh, and you are not freeloading. I enjoy having you here."

"Okay, but you have to let me help you pay some of the bills."

"I really don't need help paying anything."

"That's why I feel like a freeloader. All I've really paid for is a little bit of food and some gas. If I'm going to live here with you, then I have to help. I can either pay some directly or just pay you rent."

"I have everything set up to come directly out of my checking."

"Then I'll pay rent and what you do with it is up to you. It's either do it that way or I'll find an apartment."

Kay grabbed paper and a pen, making a rough list of monthly expenses. She turned the list so Joe could see. He looked at the list and said, "Is that everything?"

"Yes, it's just a quick estimate but I'm sure it's close."

"Then you pick a number over half. Oh, and what bank are you with? I'll set my account to automatically transfer that amount to your account the first of each month."

With that decision, Joe asked, "What's in the other garage?"

"Not much. A lawnmower and snow blower and a few yard tools."

"I have a couple of storage units where I have tools and a few other things. Can I put all that stuff in there?"

"Oh, absolutely. There's also a small storage room off the attached garage if you need it. It's pretty much empty." Looking at her watch, she said, "I need to get going. I can help you finish moving in after work."

Kay got up and headed for the door, with Joe following. Getting to her Audi A7, Joe reached and opened the door.

Stopping Kay, she turned and reached up, meeting Joe's lips as he wrapped his arms around her saying, "I'll see you later today. I'm going to start moving everything here this morning."

Giving Kay another kiss and a quick hug, he watched as she drove away. Walking back into the house, he poured another cup of coffee and called the bank. With both of them using the same bank, just different branches, it was easy, and in a few minutes, it was all done. With the first transfer today, then the first of each month from today on. Putting his cup in the sink, he headed for the storage units.

Hooking to his Toy Hauler fifth wheel camper, he loaded the rear with the first load. Arriving back home, he opened one of the overhead doors and started unloading.

With the camper empty, he backed in on the concrete pad next to the garage. Then it was back to get another load. By 3:00 p.m., he had everything in the garage and started rearranging and putting things away. Taking a dolly, he carefully moved his gun safe into the attached garage. *I had better wait till Kay gets home before putting this into the house. She might not want a safe with over thirty rifles, pistols, and shotguns in the house.*

Looking in the storage room off the attached garage, he saw a refrigerator. He checked to see if it was cold inside; he brought the tranquilizer drugs and guns there.

Then it was back to the other garage. Finding the rest of

his clothes, he carried all of them to the other garage. The pile in the center of the floor started to shrink as he found places to put things away. He looked at the south wall. *If I build shelves along that wall, I can get all of this to fit.*

Jumping back into the truck, he headed for the lumber yard just a few miles away.

With a pickup load of lumber, Joe backed up the other overhead door and got to work. Unloading and setting up for a long day of carpentry work.

He walked back inside, surveying the garage. *Shelves along that wall and a work bench here. With shelves going both ways off the bench. Plenty of room for everything. Plus, both of our vehicles should fit in the attached garage.*

With everything unloaded and some put away, plus the safe in the attached garage, Joe headed for the house to get a shower and start supper. Kay's call earlier said she would be home by six and he wanted supper ready and waiting for her.

Stopping, he looked around. Kay had about a three-acre lot with a house, attached garage, and a huge shop with a cement driveway and parking area. His rent was about the same as what he was paying for just the storage units and a place to park his camper. Smiling, he turned and walked inside.

Kay arrived home to a smiling Joe who had supper ready and waiting.

As they ate, Joe said, "I have a gun safe and over thirty guns. I would like to put it in one of the extra bedrooms and turn that room into a sort of man cave and office, with my guns and a few other things. Like a desk, filing cabinets, fax, and copy machine. You can move your desk in there also and that'll make a little more room in our room."

"That's a great idea. We can start tonight right after supper."

With both desks and the safe in the room, Joe walked to the toy hauler and started to bring in his guns. After about fifteen trips, all the guns, desk, and office equipment were in place, and they started to rearrange the bedroom.

Joe looked at the door and windows and paced the bed where he would be between Kay and anyone trying to get in or already in the house. Next, he walked back into the office. Opening the safe, he took two H&K .45s, checking to see the clips were full, he put one between the mattress and another in the top drawer of the nightstand. Telling Kay where they were, and that they were loaded.

Kay asked, "Why do you want two and why loaded?"

"It's just something I'm used to, combined with the fact that I won't sleep very well without them. I've spent way too many nights in the woods."

Kay smiled. "Okay. I know where they are, so it won't be a surprise when I see them. Oh, and by the way. There's a Rugger snub nose, 38 in the top drawer in my nightstand also."

Joe returned the smile. "Okay, I'll also clean it when I clean mine."

Kay had put water on for tea a few minutes earlier. With cups in hand, together they walked into the living room to watch a little television before bed.

The next four months were a whirlwind. The two couldn't stand being apart. Kay hated going to work; she wanted to be with Joe. Joe had to do a few short trips, ridding areas of problem animals. A contractor named Steve Davis in Arizona was trying to open a new housing area just north of Phoenix when he ran into a rattling problem. He called Joe and asked, "Can you clear an area of rattlesnakes?"

Joe replied, "Sure, although I can't promise they won't just come back."

"What if I pay you to take them twenty or more miles away and drop them off out in the desert."

"How many do you have?"

"Way too damn many." He explained what he's trying to do and where.

"Okay, I'll be there tomorrow. I'll spend a week and remove every rattler I find. I'll take them all to different areas miles from you and your project."

Joe also worked as a guide for an outfitter in Montana. He had to be gone the last half of September, all of October, and most of November doing guided hunts for elk, bighorn sheep, and mountain goats.

When the seasons finally ended, Joe couldn't get back to

Chicago and Kay fast enough. Kay took a week off at the season's end just to be with Joe after being gone for nearly two months.

One afternoon, while talking, Kay asked, "Do you like to ski?"

Joe replied, "Not really, although I'm great at drinking beer at the bar while you do."

Kay started laughing and said, "Would you try?"

Joe sat looking at the fire and said, "Sure, why not. But you'll have to be a really good teacher. I'm quite sure I'll be a very poor student. Plus, I'm likely to whine some." Pausing, he looked around and continued, "Okay, probably whine a lot."

They talked about it for a few more days and decided to do a skiing vacation in Colorado.

After a couple of days of enjoying the beauty of the Colorado mountains, one afternoon the two were walking around, doing a little shopping, when Joe disappeared for an hour.

Arriving back at their motel, Kay asked, "Where have you been?"

Joe smiled and replied, "Just looking around and setting a few things up. I talked to an outfitter and he's looking for a few new guides. I'm thinking I might do some guiding here in Colorado also. They have a huge elk herd not to mention mule deer and bighorn sheep and mountain goats."

Kay asked, "Do you need to be licensed?"

Joe took the last couple of strokes with his razor and replied, "Yes, I looked at the test. It's nearly the same as Montana's. I'm sure I can pass it with flying colors." Swatting her very shapely backside, he said, "Now get out of here so I can take a shower."

Kay smiled and reached up, giving him a kiss. She then closed the door as she walked out of the bathroom and turned on the television. She had felt the scars on his back and chest, although Joe had never removed his t-shirt in front of her or in the light. She had asked only once, and Joe replied, "Just being stupid. It's something I really don't like to talk about."

At a candlelit table that evening, having dinner, Joe looked at the dessert menu and asked, "This cinnamon apple dessert looks really good. Would you like to share one?"

"Oh my God, that does look scrumptious."

Joe caught the waiter's eyes and ordered one. Their waiter, Terry, glanced at Joe and, with a simple nod, Terry knew what to do. As he placed the dessert in front her, the surprise was evident as her eyes and mouth flew open. There was a beautiful marquise cut diamond engagement ring on top.

Joe looked at her, waiting for a response. Kay had tears running down both cheeks. All she could do was nod.

They married two months later in a private ceremony in a small country church by Pastor Nicki Meyer. Joe's best friend, Logan, was his best man, along with Adrian and Colton, for groomsmen. Kay's best friend, Heather, was the maid of honor, along with Rene and her daughter, Alicia, for bridesmaids, with just family and a few close friends attending.

That night, after dinner and a little dancing at the restaurant and bar connected to the hotel, they all sat down and had a few more drinks. A smorgasbord of appetizers was put out, and they simply enjoyed the rest of the evening.

After everyone had been talking for a couple of hours, Joe looked around and said, "Good night, folks." He reached over and picked up his new bride.

Kay screamed as Joe held her, saying, "Put me down!"

Joe laughed. "Oh no, you're never getting away from me!" Smiling, he continued, "We have a new life together, and it starts tonight."

Kay wrapped her arms around Joe, looking back at family and friends, and said, "I guess I'll be seeing you all in the morning!"

Everyone started clapping as he carried her to the room.

Kissing her gently, he lay her down on the bed

Chapter Nine

Standing in the FBO now, they both knew it would be a couple of months before they would be together again. After Joe finished there, he had to head for the Yukon Territory in Canada and live trap a polar bear that was terrifying a village on the Arctic Ocean. Canadian officials did not want to kill the bear and hired Joe to trap it and relocate it.

Joe and Kay stood there, sipping coffee and talking as the pilot walked in and said, "There's a small break in the overcast, I'm sure we can get out, although we have to go now."

Being a pilot himself, Joe walked over and looked at the radar and weather report. He saw the small hole that was supposed to get larger as it approached the mountains.

Together, while holding hands, Joe and Kay followed the pilot toward the waiting plane. Joe walked around the plane, looking at a few different things, moving the ailerons, elevator, and rudder. Then, giving her one more hug and kiss, he helped her in, making sure her seatbelts were secure. Reaching for the controls, Joe turned and pulled on the yoke, checking the ailerons and elevator. Looking at Kay, he said, "Step on that pedal. I just want to see the rudder move."

Kay stepped on the rudder as Joe turned back to her and

smiled, and then reaching up, he kissed her one more time and closed the door. Walking away, he got a feeling that something terrible was about to happen. It was the same feeling he got in Afghanistan when all hell was about to break loose. Stopping, he looked at the surrounding mountains, then turned and looked at Kay. He smiled. *I'm sure it's just my nerves. I simply don't want her to leave.*

That terrible feeling was still there. There was no denying it. Something was about to go wrong, although he did not know what. He saw the break in the weather and the forecast. He could now visibly see the hole they were going to fly through. He watched as the plane lifted off and climbed out until it was out of sight. Wiping the tears from his eyes, he walked toward his pickup. He was missing her already. Getting back to their motel room, he sat on the bed. He could still smell her perfume.

That terrible feeling was *still* there, although he had no idea why or what it was about. Kay was going home. The last two weeks had been a blast, and he hated to see her leave.

Shaking his head, he started packing and going through his equipment, trying to shake that feeling off. As he did, his phone rang.

Joe reached for his phone, saying, "Hello."

The voice on the phone asked, "Is this Joe West?"

Joe replied, "Yes, it is."

"This is Steve from the airport," said the voice, "I have bad news. Can you come back here right away? We have an ELT transmitting, and it's registered to the plane your wife just left in."

Oh my God, oh my God, why would the emergency locator transmitter be triggered? He ran to his pickup. Going through town, Joe slowed, then drove through two stoplights and a stop sign. As the town police officer took off after him, Joe never slowed down. Arriving at the airport, the officer hollered, "Hey, you, stop right there!"

Turning, Joe answered him, saying, "I don't have time for your shit right now. If you want to talk to me, follow and wait your turn." He ran into the airport.

Finding the pilot's briefing room, he looked from one to the other as he said, "I'm Joe West. What's going on? What happened? What can you tell me?"

Just then, the officer walked in. Grabbing Joe, he tried to push him against the wall. Joe sidestepped the attempt. Grabbing the officer by the arm, he pivoted and pushed the officer's face first against the wall and said, "I told you to wait. The plane where my wife is in has possibly crashed. I'll talk to you as soon as I can. Although right now, I have more important things to deal with."

The officer stepped back and said, "Whoa, stop. I'm Brad Davis. I'm on search and rescue. What happened and how long ago?"

Steve walked over to the map, pointing, he said, "The ELT

says the airplane is about here. The GPS confirms its location. It hasn't moved for about thirty minutes. I'm quite sure it's crashed. We have tried to call them on the radio. They should be able to receive us but there's been no reply. We've called the FAA. They have not heard from them. Plus, there was no mayday called out that anyone has heard. So, there is nothing they can do until this weather breaks."

Joe walked to the window and looked at the snow-capped mountains. Turning, he said, "Write that transmitting location down, along with another information that comes in. I'll be back in an hour."

Walking out the door, he headed back to his motel room, thinking. *Kay's plane had crashed in the mountains. From what I saw, it was above the timberline.*

Arriving at the motel, he started checking his equipment, making a list of what else he might need.

Sitting down, he took a couple of deep breaths, trying to clear his mind. Looking at the list, he added a few more items. Grabbing his belt, he strapped on his pistol along with ammunition and a knife. Picking up his backpack, he started packing everything he thought he could possibly need.

One more glance at the list, he picked up the pack and walked out. Throwing the pack in the back of the truck, he headed for the only sporting goods store in town.

Pausing, he looked at his reflection. Picking up his phone, he called a Montana number. Logan answered, saying, "Hey buddy, what part of the world are you in now?"

Joe replied, "I'm in Alaska."

"Now what, pray tell, are you doing up there besides screwing off."

Joe says, "Logan, I'm going to ask you a huge favor. Kay and I have been vacationing and she left an hour ago. Logan, her plane just went down in the Wrangle Saint Alias mountains. I've talked to everyone I can find, and it looks like search and rescue is headed up there in the morning."

Logan's reply was instant. "Joe, I'll be there in the morning. I can catch a flight out of Billings to Anchorage. Then bush plane to you. Give me your GPS location."

Joe answered, "Sorry, Logan. I can't wait that long, and besides, the weather won't allow that. The rescue helicopters are grounded because of the weather. You are my absolute best friend. I would not ask this of just anyone. There's a sporting goods store here. I'm going to leave a map of the area with Kay's location and the route I'm going to use. I'll mark my trail with axe marks in the trees along the way. If I don't call you in a week, find Kay's and my body and bring us out. We both want to be cremated and buried together. Logan, we want to be in the mountains."

Logan replied, "Absolutely and how about on my ranch. Say that valley west of the house? On that bluff overlooking the lake."

"That would be perfect and thanks, Logan. I'll call you by

next Thursday."

Walking into the store, Joe grabbed the things he needed and said, "Hey, Darrel. I don't know if you heard but Kay's plane went down." Pointing out the window, he continued, "Up there. I'm leaving now, taking the forest service road to the logging road. From the end, I'll go on foot. A friend of mine will be here in eight days if I don't call him. If I fail to get her out and if search and rescue doesn't get us out, he will. He's going to ask you for this." He handed Darrel the envelope with all the information in it.

Darrel replied, "Call him back and tell him it's under the till drawer. That way, anyone can get it for him."

Joe reached out and shook Darrel's hand. "Thank you."

Turning, he walked out the door only to stop and walk back to the counter. "I need to pay for these supplies."

"Get out of here. We can catch up when you get back. Go get your wife."

As Joe walked away, Darrel said, "I'm leaving with the rescue team in the morning." Throwing him a radio, he said, "Keep in touch, and Joe, I pray she's alive."

Joe stopped and wiped his eyes. Turning and looking at the mountains, he said, "Yeah, me too. Me too."

He then raced back to the airport. As he spoke with Steve and Bob about getting the GPS location of the emergency transmitter, he called search and rescue. Brad answered the phone saying, "Search and rescue, this is Brad."

"Hi Brad, sorry about earlier today."

"Not a problem. I would have done the same thing." Pausing for a minute, he continued, "The weather has the helicopter grounded. It's not expected to lift for forty-eight to seventy-two hours."

Joe swore under his breath. *If anyone is alive, if Kay is alive, she will not be in that length of time.*

Joe said, "What is search and rescue planning?"

"We are getting a rescue team together now and plan on leaving before the first light tomorrow morning."

"I know the area. I've spent a lot of time up there looking for that damn bear. I'm headed up that way now. I'll mark my trail by slashing tree bark, making it easy for you to follow."

Joe walked outside and looked at the rugged mountains. The valley he was in was about two thousand feet above sea level. The mountains in that area were in the eleven-thousand-foot area, with some over sixteen thousand feet. As he looked at the jagged, snow-covered peaks, he knew this was going to test everything he had.

Kay was up there somewhere. All he knew was she needed him. He would find her, and nothing would stand in his way. There was no way he could wait until morning. He knew she was alive, and he was going to get her out. He would not accept the idea that she was dead. Not Kay, never, not the only woman he had ever loved.

Joe drove out of town and headed for a logging or forestry

road he knew that twisted and climbed several miles up the mountain. Arriving at the road, it was gated shut. In a matter of a few minutes, with the help of two chains, the gate was open and laying on the ground. Joe threw both chains back in the pickup. Driving over the twisted gate, he started up the road that would eventually lead him to Kay.

He would find her and bring her out. She was alive; he just knew it. He had promised to protect her at all costs, and now, he felt like he had let her down. Coming to the end of the mountain road, he thought of Kay up there, probably hurt and very scared. That thought alone drove him forward.

He packed his climbing equipment, including a small tent that could double as a suspension or hanging platform in case he was stuck climbing and could not reach the top before dark, making sure he had two sleeping bags, a couple of tanks of camp fuel, food, and water.

Pausing, he grabbed the first aid kit, opening it, he checked to see if he still had that pain medication a doctor had given him along with extra ammunition for the two guns he carried. A .44 Magnum pistol loaded with 300-grain hollow points and a .300 Winchester Short Mag in a Model 70 mountain rifle loaded with 240-grain hollow points.

Getting everything ready, he strapped on the backpack, picked up the rifle, and headed up into the mountains, marking his trail as he climbed. He knew there was a game trail that twisted around the mountain and headed up, although that would take three days of hard climbing to where Kay was. That was simply too long. As he hiked, he noticed a paw print.

"Awww, shit," he said. "There's a grizzly in the area." He could tell by the paw print it was a large bear.

As he walked, he thought about the bear causing the problem. The fact it had outsmarted him a couple of times. He wondered if it was that bear. He knew a grizzly could smell blood from miles away. If there was blood, and he knew there would be. It was Kay's blood that bear was tracking. It could be headed in the same direction up the mountain. Now, time was of the essence. He had to hurry. People are not on a grizzlies' normal food list, although they have been known to kill and eat people. He had to get to Kay, and fast. She was not going to be a bear's next meal.

Joe quickened his step and started climbing. *A straight line between two points is the shortest distance.* He was in great shape, six foot and two hundred pounds. He could climb at this pace for a long time, although the weight in his backpack would slow him down some. He needed that equipment. There was no choice; he had to carry it. He figured he should be there sometime late the next afternoon.

At the base of a three-hundred-foot rock wall, he looked in both directions. It seemed to go on forever. He knew this wall ran all the way to where the game trail cut straight uphill, so he started looking for a climbing route. Seeing a crack that ran up the face, he thought, *That looks like the best route.*

Setting up for the climb, he looked uphill. Kay was up there somewhere. About two hundred feet up the wall, he knew he would not make the top before dark, and climbing after dark was not a good idea.

He started setting up a hanging camp, double and triple checking all the ropes. Making absolutely sure they were all tied off correctly. If one broke, it could become a real problem. Joe sat there as he made a cold supper and then tried to get some sleep. All he could do was think of Kay. She had to be alive.

Laying down, Joe let his mind drift.

He was running from the Taliban, climbing up the side of a cliff, not as steep as the one he was climbing now. Although certain of death if he fell. Bullets started hitting around him. Only ten feet to the shelf as one hit the rocks only inches away. They were walking their shots closer and closer. Not just spraying bullets on full automatic and hoping to hit something. With only two feet to go, he felt something hit his backpack. With his hand on the edge of the shelf, he rolled over and found cover. With bullets striking above and below, he thought, *Time to even the odds. Maybe if I can kill a few, that should slow their approach and I can get over the top and disappear.* Carefully, he slid the barrel over the edge and sighted downhill. He could see several men moving from rock to rock as they worked their way uphill toward him.

He was on his own. Totally alone, but that's how he wanted

it. Do or die, it was his decision. Outnumbered and outgunned. He had to even the odds. He watched for a minute or two. Until one man showed he might be the leader of this gang of goat herders and placed the crosshairs on his chest. No fancy head shots now. He didn't care if they died instantly, as long as they died.

By using 122-grain full metal jacketed boat tail ammunition, it should penetrate most light body armor. The guy stood, and he squeezed the trigger. The man was slammed backwards into a huge rock. A red streak appeared as he slid to the ground.

He continued to watch and placed every shot where it had to be. He had the high ground and slowly, the gang of goat herders started retreating. With the use of his range finder, a couple more never got off the mountain. Waiting to make sure they were in full retreat, he finished climbing. Slowly, he worked his way along the ledge and over the top. In an hour, he was five miles away and headed for his hidden camp. High on the side of another mountain with over-hanging cliffs. A place he could defend and had two escape routes. One was going up by climbing through a chimney and over the top. Joe had secured a rope at the top. Make his escape that way easier and faster. The other went down and around and then up.

Taking his pack off, he found what had saved his life. A bible he carried had a slug in it. The bullet had made it nearly through but had stopped. Carefully, he removed the bullet and placed the Bible back in the same spot. Looking to the heavens, he said, "Thank you."

Just before 2 a.m., Joe woke with a start. Panicked and breathing deeply, he shook his head, trying to clear the dream.

"Wow," he said aloud.

The nightmares and dreams are so real, reliving the past in his dreams. He could feel the warm trails of blood running down his chest where he had been shot. Lifting his shirt, he looked at the old wounds. Taking a deep breath, he tried to calm down.

There was another storm blowing in, rocking, and swaying his hanging camp. He was tied off about two hundred feet in the air, with the wind blowing everything back and forth. He continued to check and recheck the ropes, trying to make sure nothing would break. He needed almost everything he had. After an hour or so, the storm had blown through, and he was able to get a few more hours of sleep.

At first light, he was again checking his equipment. Everything was there except his rifle. He looked through the tent one more time. Then, looking down, he could see it lying on the rocks below. Somehow, the rifle had slid out of the hanging tent. He knew he would need that rifle, but now, it was one less thing to carry.

As he hung by his lifeline, he packed up his camp and started climbing. Kay was up there, and he was going to get to be at her side today. He had to get to her. She was alive. He could feel it; he just knew it.

By mid-morning, with new energy, he finished the climb. He knew he was going to bring her out this way, so he left his climbing equipment there. His backpack was lighter. He headed out again, making better time. He checked his GPS and could tell she was about four thousand feet above him still. That was a full day at this altitude, he figured. He was now about 7,500 feet above sea level, about half the oxygen there was at sea level. Climbing on adrenaline and fear, he was at the crash site just before dark.

Chapter Ten

The pilot was dead, but Kay was alive. Barely alive, but alive. Joe looked to the heavens with tears running down his cheeks and said, "Oh God, thank you. She's alive. She's still alive."

He had done the impossible. He had climbed almost 11,500 vertical feet in two days and found Kay still alive. Clearing the tears from his eyes, carefully and slowly, he got her out of the wreckage.

He looked at her injuries, and getting the first aid kit, he bandaged her up the best he could. Then, he started getting her into the sleeping bag. Making a hot camp using the camp fuel, he made her some tea, adding a painkiller to it. He sat with Kay's head in his lap as he slowly got her to sip on the tea. Next, he made them a quick supper. Again, he held her in his lap, trying to get some warm food and more tea into her. She drifted in and out of consciousness, but he did manage to get her to eat and drink some. Mostly, he wanted to get the pain medication into her.

She held his hand and with tears in her eyes, she whispered, "I knew you would come. I just knew it. I held on. I just wanted to see you one more time. That's what kept me alive; wanting to just see you again. I love you, Joe. I love you so very much."

Joe looked down at his wife and replied, "I love you, too. I'm here now, so relax. I'll get you out of here and I'll never let anything, or anyone ever hurt you again."

Carefully, he bent forward and kissed her on the forehead and then the lips. As he watched, Kay slipped back into unconsciousness.

Joe checked her pulse continuously throughout the night. Rearranging everything, he got into his sleeping bag. Then, carefully, he pulled her back into his lap.

Sitting there with Kay in his lap, he slowly stroked her hair as he said, "I have something I have to tell you. I had a life you know nothing about. I spent four years in Afghanistan. I was a sniper with the US Special Forces. After that, with my military training, I went to work for the DEA. I spent ten years in the jungles of Colombia. Gathering Intel and relaying it to a handler in the US. They would set up and stop the drugs coming in by plane or boat. I'd get them tail numbers of the planes and the type of boat headed across the gulf."

Joe would drift off, only to wake a few minutes later and check on Kay. Making sure she was still alive. Finally, he drifted off to a very restless night.

He was lying on his stomach in a brush. They had found him, but how? He never followed the same trail and had always checked his back trail. He could feel the weight of the snake as it crawled across his back. From the weight and length, he was sure it was a Bushmaster, one of the most venomous snakes in South America. He knew if it bit him, he would never be able to lie still, and the patrol from the cartel would kill him. Bullets or venom, dead was dead, although the bullets would save him from a slow, painful death. Slowly, he felt the snake leave his back. Scared to move for fear of the deadly snake bite and the patrol, Randy laid perfectly still. Soon, the patrol started moving off.

As quietly as possible, Randy slipped down the bank into the river. It was nearly dark, and his only chance was to slowly float downstream for a couple of miles. He felt as if the anaconda jaws closed on his leg. Slowly, the coils started encircling him. While his hands were still loose, Randy's hand found his knife and, taking a deep breath, he slipped underwater. He felt as the coils continued to encircle him, slowly tightening their grip. With his hands still free, he grabbed behind the snake's head. Randy placed the knife under and between its jaws and pushed up and in. The snake gave one massive tremor and was dead. Randy moved the knife in a circle, cutting away the snake behind its head. He could feel as the coils loosened their grip and started falling away. Slowly, he surfaced, then looking around, he continued to float with the current. Knowing there were caimans and more likely other anacondas in the area, he knew he would have to get out of the water as soon as possible.

Slowly, he made his way across the river to the far bank.

Working his way out of the river and up the bank, he found a place. Sitting down with the help of his knife, he started removing the snake's head and teeth from his lower leg.

As the sun rose, he woke up. Shaking his head to try to clear the dreams. He made coffee for himself, plus some breakfast. He also made tea and a warm mashed-up breakfast for Kay. He knew she needed to eat. The trip down would be hard on her, too. He knew today would start a test that held her life in his ability. He had to get Kay to the hospital. He grabbed his radio and called search-and-rescue. The ground team had left early that day and was coming up the game trail.

Joe knew it would be two days before they got there. Very possibly longer if they had any trouble. He tried to call the ground team over and over, to no avail. Then he tried calling anyone who might be listening. *They were probably on the back side of the mountain and more than likely in that ravine. If so, they would have no reception*, thought Joe. Walking to the plane, he picked up the radio mic and tried reaching the airport by saying, "Can anyone hear me?"

Waiting a few seconds, he tried again. He then keyed the mic several times. Listening, he heard nothing, not even static. Bumping the switch, he could tell there was absolutely no electricity in the plane. The battery had probably broken on impact.

Pausing to think, he knew he could not wait. If he did, it would take them too long to get there. By the time they got to where he was now, he would be off the wall and going through the forest, and on a much gentler slope. He packed his equipment and, by using a couple of long slender poles and parts of the plane, he made a travois to pull Kay to the wall.

He also pulled the pilot out and carried him over to a large boulder. Carefully, he stacked rocks around him and on top of him until he had him covered with a couple of layers. Then, taking a couple of sticks, he made a makeshift cross. This would mark the spot for the search and rescue. Hopefully, it would also keep any scavengers away until the rescue team got there to bring him out.

Next, he started getting her into the travois and got her secured. Double checking the way he had strapped her into the travois. Standing there, he took a deep breath. *I sure hope this works.* Bending, he softly kissed her. Picking up the poles, he finally headed down the mountain.

Going down was harder than the climb. There were areas where he pulled her and areas where he had to let her down with the only length of rope he had. When he was pulling Kay, he watched for loose rocks that could trip him up or anything else that could cause a problem. If he got hurt, they were both in real trouble.

The terrain was rough, and he had to make sure he did not lose control or have the thing push him over, going down the steep slope. Several times, he had to stop to secure Kay and then walk down and roll rocks out of the way or change direction to find a way to go around larger rocks and boulders. Then climb back up and start down again. Late that day, he finally made it to the wall.

Making a camp, he again made a fast meal and tea. He needed high carb, high-calorie foods to restore what he had used. As he ate, he also tried to feed Kay. She needed liquid to keep her blood pressure up and to keep as warm as possible to try to keep her from going into shock. Keeping her alive was all that mattered. He checked her injuries, making sure that what he had done was still in place. He laid the hanging tent on the ground, picked up Kay, and placed her on it. He put more wood on the fire, and he crawled into his sleeping bag. Rearranging Kay until she was in his lap. Then he started to stroke her hair as he told her about his secret life. He drifted in and out of sleep, waking several times to check on her.

When sleep finally came, he was back in Afghanistan.

He was lying on a rock shelf. He could see several groups moving through the valley below. Suddenly, a call came across his earpiece. A call out for help. A small patrol had been hit earlier and were trying to get back to base. They ran into a large force of Taliban fighters. Randy heard as they asked for either artillery or air support. Randy answered, saying, "This is the ghost. I'm in the area, repeat, I'm in the area and beyond where the squad is. I can assist and give cover fire."

The call came back saying, "Too late ghost, take cover, artillery is inbound. Repeat artillery is inbound."

Randy heard the incoming shells as he ran for the cover of a ravine, as the first hit two hundred yards below him. Knocking him off his feet, he yelled into his radio, "Cease fire, repeat, cease fire, damn it. I'm beyond the patrol, and you'll shell me." Getting back to his feet, he continued to run for the ravine just as the last of the shells hit. Behind him, blowing him over the edge and into the ravine. Laying there dazed and confused, he slowly gathered his wits and started to climb to a location where he could get a better look at what was happening.

Sighting down on the group of fighters, he touched the trigger. A pink mist covered the rock directly in front of where the Taliban fighter had been hiding. Randy continued to pick targets and watched as the patrol started advancing. Between his cover fire from above and behind and the patrol going on the offensive, the fight was over in a few minutes. All eighteen of the Taliban were either dead, wounded, or taken prisoner. Randy picked up his radio and contacted the patrol by saying, "Red dog one, this is ghost. Do you guys need any more assistance?"

The reply was instant, "Ghost, this is Red dog one. Thanks for your help. We are good. Repeat, thanks, we are good. You really saved our bacon. Red dog one out."

Randy replied, "Red dog one, this is ghost. You are most

welcome. Glad I was in the area. Ghost out."

Before sunrise, he was up, making breakfast and coffee. He felt restless, although he did not remember the dream. Next, he made tea for Kay. Again, he tried to feed her and get her to drink some tea with the painkiller in it. He could tell she was getting weaker. He held her hand as she looked at him. He could see the pain in her eyes as the tears started again.

She whispered, "I love you."

He had to turn away. His eyes were also full of tears. He knew the next several hours would be the test. One slip, and everything was over. He set up the equipment to lower Kay to the base of the wall. He checked and rechecked all the ropes, making sure there was no chance of something breaking or going wrong. Putting Kay in the hanging tent and attaching the ropes, he rechecked them repeatedly. Throwing the rope over the side of the cliff, he eased her over the edge and started lowering her.

Everything was going as planned, but with about a hundred feet to go, the only thing he could not check became tangled. The rope he had thrown over the side had developed a knot and was stuck. He pulled on it several times with no luck. It was stuck.

"Not now!" he screamed. "Not now!"

Using every muscle he had, he pulled her up just enough to get the rope into a locking clevis. This would allow the rope to be held there so he could go down the rope that held Kay and try to undo the knot. As he rappelled down the wall, he saw the problem.

He tried to get the knot undone, but it was not happening. Only one choice was left: he had to cut the rope below the knot, then reattach the rope above the knot using a Machard mountaineering knot, then cut the rope again between the knot, and where he reattached it. If this worked, his weight would hold her from a hundred or so foot drop to the jagged rocks below. As he worked, he knew that if he failed, they would both die.

After getting everything ready and rechecking the knot he had tied, he looked down at Kay, then up to the heavens. He knew if she fell, he would cut his rope and follow her. Then, taking both ropes in his hand, he took a deep breath.

Again, he looked at his wife and said, "I love you more than life."

He looked up into the heavens, and leaning back, putting tension on his lifeline, he cut both ropes. It held; it worked.

"Wow!" he screamed, letting out his breath.

The knot had held.

He then tied a quick knot at the end of the cut rope. One more quick safety feature: if the other knot he had tied started to slip, this would stop it.

Now, with his weight holding her from falling and her weight lifting him as he climbed, she was safely at the base of the wall in a short time. He quickly climbed the last hundred feet or so, grabbed his gear, lowered it, and retied the rope and made a fast descent on the wall. They were down. Joe sat down on a rock and took his first breath that wasn't full of fear in days. She was safe and almost out. He could not believe it; he had gotten Kay halfway down. Just one more day, and she would be in the hospital and getting the medical attention she needed.

He looked for the radio to call the ground search-and-rescue team. The radio was gone.

"Oh, no!" he yelled. "What's next?"

He then frantically looked everywhere for the radio. It was not there; it must have fallen out somewhere. Again, he started making camp—better to stay there that night. There was plenty of wood and shelter from the wind in the rocks. Besides, he needed the rest. His body was getting really sore. He made a hot meal for himself and Kay, and some tea for both. He put more painkillers in the tea. What she would not drink, he would. He was sore along with being both mentally and physically exhausted. After eating, he started getting Kay comfortable. He then covered himself with the other sleeping bag. Rearranging Kay, he said, "Honey, I have to tell you more about a part of me you know nothing about."

Joe started, "While I was in Afghanistan, I watched as one of our patrols was ambushed. I was above them and about a half mile away. It was a hell of a fight. I could see our guys.

They were pinned down and getting piss pounded. There was no one else in that area, so no help was coming, as I moved, trying to get close enough to join the fight. From my vantage point, I could see our troops getting killed. I was above them and behind the Taliban. I finally got to the point where I could get into the fight and give high ground cover support. I had taken several shots when I saw a couple trying to get above me. One guy saw me and fired. More of a spray and pray. Just hold the trigger down until he was out of ammunition. Anyway, one of his shots hit me high in the shoulder just above my body armor. That was the first time I had been shot. I saw the muscle flash and knew I was hit before my brain could register the pain. It was my right shoulder, so it didn't affect my shooting much. Soon, the Taliban started to back out. The US troops continued to pursue them but broke off when I radioed I had been hit. I spent three days in the hospital and four weeks in camp on medical relief. I was supposed to stay longer but I snuck out with a patrol. The following morning, after I broke off, my radio came to life. I listened but never replied. That doctor and the camp commander were really pissed. Although I was also a commander so there wasn't much they could do besides yell."

Soon, Joe drifted off to sleep. His sleep was full of broken dreams of both Afghanistan and Colombia. Snakes, bullets, men who were trying to find and kill him. Swamps and mountains dealing death and destruction.

Again and again, he woke up.

Each time, he would lay perfectly still until his senses knew there was no danger in the area. Then, he would check on her. Looking at her lying there was the hardest thing. She was always so full of life, always on the move and doing something. She couldn't die now. She just couldn't. With just a little luck, she would be in the hospital by this time tomorrow.

As the sun rose, he woke up.

Again, he made coffee for himself and tea for Kay. He added a painkiller to Kay's tea. He was still sore, although Kay needed it more. He made a quick breakfast and also fed Kay as she lay in his lap, and he stroked her hair, telling her they were almost out. He packed up everything he needed, leaving the climbing equipment. He would come back later or ask the rescue team to pick it up. Either way, he did not need it anymore, although he did grab the tent and two lengths of rope.

In the tent, he placed on the travois again to support Kay, making it a little more comfortable for her. After making sure everything was done and packed. Reaching for his pistol, he checked it was fully loaded. That damn bear might still be around.

He started down, pulling the travois. It was hard going. There were large trees and rocks to go around. After a couple of hours, he could hear something moving, although he could not see it. The forest was getting thicker, so he decided it might be easier to carry her.

He repacked what he thought he might need and picked up his wife, tenderly kissing her cheek. As far as he was concerned, there wasn't another woman in the world. With Kay in his arms, he started walking. This was by far easier, and they made good time, the pack on his back acting like a counterbalance.

He heard something moving and stopped.

There was something out there, but what?

He knew if that bear charged, he would have to act quickly. Although he also knew he could not drop her. Then it happened, a deer broke cover and ran straight at him.

Wow! That scared the shit out of me!

He continued walking, and with his senses sharp, he hoped he would hear or smell danger.

Bears give off a very distinctive odor. Nursing females have a sour milk smell, while males usually smell like carrion or rotten meat. This one smelled like the dump in town. He continued down the trail and came around the corner.

The bear broke out the brush and charged.

He tried to get out of the way, but the bear hit them. As he fell, he kept Kay on top, giving her some protection from the fall. He quickly rolled over, keeping her tight against him. As he did, he reached for his pistol.

The bear had Joe's leg in his mouth and was starting to bite down. He tried to shoot as the bear shook him, jarring the pistol out of his hand. The bear let go and turning; it looked in Kay's direction. Joe looked around frantically, saw the pistol lying in the leaves about five feet away. As the bear walked toward Kay, he scrambled for the pistol and yelled, getting the bear's attention. Again, it charged. He grabbed the pistol and spun, taking a quick aim, and fired.

The 300-grain hollow point hit the bear in the front shoulder. A crippling shot, but not fatal. As the bear ran off, Joe got one more shot off he thought might have hit it, although he wasn't totally sure where.

Opening the cylinder, he reloaded the two empty spots and slid one more into the space under the hammer he normally left empty. He then crawled to Kay, making sure she was okay, then finding the first aid kit, he poured hydrogen peroxide on his leg, then wrapped it with a pressure bandage, all while continuing to watch the brush in all directions. After doing the best he could with what he had, he took a couple of pain pills. Then turned his attention back to Kay.

He had a really big problem. There was a wounded grizzly in the area, while Kay needed medical attention. If the bear attacked again, they might not be so lucky. If he got hurt any worse than what he was now, there would be no way he could carry her out.

Looking around, he rigged the hanging tent and threw

ropes over large tree branches and hoisted Kay clear of danger. He had to make sure she was protected at all costs.

Now, thinking back, he thought he had noticed it missing an eye and an ear. It was the bear that was causing all the trouble around the area.

Then double checking the cylinder in his pistol to make sure it was loaded, he started after the bear. After tracking it for some distance, he paused, looking around.

"Damn," Joe said. "That damn bear is circling. I'm quite sure I've walked through this area once already."

Turning, Joe picked up the pace to get back to where he had left his wife and to get her to safety. Then and only then would he come back after that damn bear.

About thirty minutes later, he was back. Kay needed him more. As he walked, he looked and listened very carefully for anything that could be out there. He carefully lowered her down. Then quickly, he packed everything back up. Strapping on the backpack, he reached down and picked up his wife. Being careful not to move her head very much, and started out.

They had gone about two miles, and his leg was killing him. He carefully laid Kay down and stood up.

Just as the bear broke cover and charged again.

This time, his hands were empty. Grabbing his pistol from the holster as he dove sideways.

Yelling as he came back to his feet, "Hey dumb ass, I'm

back here. You missed me!"

The bear spun around and charged again.

He waited until the last possible second and stepped backward behind a tree, firing four shots at nearly point-blank range. Watching as the bear ran down the trail and disappeared into the brush.

He was sure he had hit it at least three times. About thirty yards away, it walked back onto the trail. Joe was still trying to reload as the bear turned his way. The huge carnivore stood there looking at him and sniffed the air. It had tasted blood and could smell blood. Slowly, it started back toward him. Joe took aim and fired three times. Hitting the bear twice, he knew he had rushed his first shot. The bear spun and disappeared back into the woods.

Watching where it had vanished into the trees, he knew he had to finish it. He could not leave a wounded animal to suffer. He finished reloading as he limped back to Kay's side. He kneeled down and said, "I'll be back, it's badly wounded, and I need to finish this. I can't leave a wounded bear in the area, and I don't want it tracking us."

Kay whispered, "I'll wait right here."

Dropping onto both knees, he gently kissed her, stroking her hair, he said, "I love you."

Standing, he turned and walked away. Armed only with a pistol, Joe was hunting one of the largest carnivores in North America.

He had walked only about sixty yards when the bear broke cover and charged. Spinning and trying to take careful aim, he started shooting, hitting the bear four more times. The bear hit Joe like a runaway freight train, knocking him to the side and falling over dead. Joe used his good leg to push himself away and behind a tree as he reloaded. Then, standing, he limped towards it and from about ten feet he put five more bullets in it.

Quickly, he then reloaded and waited.

After about fifteen minutes, he picked up a long stick, then carefully limped up and poked it several times in the back. It never moved. The damn thing was dead.

He checked its head one more time to make sure it had a missing eye and an ear.

Yes, it did.

This was the bear he had come to Alaska to either capture or kill.

He leaned backwards against a tree. Taking a deep breath, he slowly slid down the tree to the ground. Breathing deeply, he turned sideways and fell over backward. "Wow," he said "Oh, my God, it's over. It's finally over."

Joe lay there in the grass for a few minutes. Then, slowly, he got up and looked. The bear was dead and less than ten yards from where Kay lay.

Being true to her word, she was still there. He put on the backpack, and picking up his wife, he started again. His leg was getting worse all the time. Now, he was going on pure adrenaline. He knew the pickup was still about five miles away. As he continued down the trail in its direction, he had to stop and rest frequently. Checking his leg, he could see where it had started bleeding through the bandage. Looking at Kay, then down the trail, he knew he had to stop. He had to stop the bleeding and fix the dressing, pouring the rest of the hydrogen peroxide on the bite. Then he took several of the largest sterile pads, smearing liberal amounts of triple antibiotic cream on them, he then placed them on the area around the bite. Then wrapped it with gauze and finally, he added the pressure wrap.

Bending down, he kissed Kay. Picking her up, he started out.

This time, he made the truck.

Chapter Eleven

He carefully placed Kay in the back seat and did his best to strap her in. Walking around the truck, he stopped and put his hands on the hood. Standing there, he took several deep breaths and looked to the heavens, and silently, he said, "Thank you for giving me the strength to save her. I guess you know what she means to me."

Climbing in, he started down the mountain road towards town and the hospital. The trip down the mountain road was rough, filled with holes and washouts. Stopping several times, he would roll large rocks in the washed-out areas. More than once, he got stuck and had to back up and fill the washout with more rocks, large chunks of wood, and whatever he could find and carry.

About ten miles down the road, the bridge had washed out. He put the truck in four-wheel drive and started crossing the river, with the current moving fast. At first, he wasn't sure if he would make it. The tires spun and caught, then spun some more, with Joe turning the wheel back and forth. Shifting from low to reverse and back to low while continuing to turn the steering wheel back-and-forth, mixed with a little swearing and a lot of praying. The tires finally found the traction they needed, and they started up the far bank.

Just two miles from town, a tree laid fallen across the road.

Joe got out, limping around the truck. He opened the toolbox as he reached for his chainsaw, when he spotted the chains he had used to open the gate.

Grabbing the chain, he wrapped it around the tree and hooked it on the tow hooks. Putting the pickup in reverse, he pushed the gas pedal to the floor. With a squealing of tires, the tree slid across the road and out of the way. Jumping out, he unhooked it from the truck. Dropping the chain where he stood, he headed for town.

***

Stopping in front of the main entrance at the hospital, he left the engine running as he ran to the passenger side. A man called out, "Hey, you can't park there!"

Joe just ignored the man as he picked Kay up and walked through the front doors, yelling, "Help me. Someone, please help me."

A doctor and two nurses came running, one grabbing a gurney.

They could not believe what they saw. Joe, bruised, bloody and limping and carrying Kay, stopping just inside the front door. Joe carefully placed Kay on the gurney with tears running down both cheeks. He bent forward, kissing her tenderly. "You are safe honey, you are safe." Joe leaned backwards against the wall and slowly slid to the floor.

Four hours later, he woke up and called out, "Nurse, hey, someone, anyone. Where's my wife? Where's Kay?"

He got up, pulling out the IV and wires. He limped down the hall to find her.

A nurse ran up and said, "You need to get back in bed. You're not well enough to be walking around."

Joe ignored her as he continued to walk from room to room, looking for Kay. He found her in the room right next to the nurse's station. She had all sorts of tubes and wires hooked to her.

A few seconds later, Doctor Adam Swenson walked in. Looking at Joe standing there, he said, "She's in a coma. We have run a few tests and have more to run. She has brain activity and is alive. That's all I can tell you for now. She is on life support, although she is breathing on her own. Without what you had done, there is no doubt she would be dead."

Joe's eyes instantly filled with tears as he walked to his wife's side. Stopping, he pulled up a chair, sitting down, he picked up her hand.

Doctor Adam said, "You need to be in your room."

Through tear-filled eyes, Joe looked at him and said, "I am in my room. I'm not leaving her. If you need me, this is where I'll be."

Later that day, Joe called Kay's parents and kids, repeating the story several times but leaving out most of the details. He told them how she was. He called every day as he watched his wife slowly get worse.

The fourth afternoon, the doctor came in as Joe sat with

Kay. He was holding her hand and stroking her hair when the doctor said, "The weather is still bad, and the Life Flight helicopter cannot get in, nor could the rescue helicopter get out. The only road leaving was closed. The bridge had washed away. It looks like we are trapped."

Joe looked down at his wife and said, "I've been talking with your folks and kids. They are as worried as I am. As soon as this weather breaks, I'll get you out of here. These people are doing all they can. But you need to be relocated to a bigger hospital where they have the equipment for what you need."

All he could think of was Kay. She could not have survived everything just to die in the hospital. With tears running down his face, he continued to hold her hand, stroke her hair, and talk to her. Several times, Dr. Swenson or one of the nurses came in to check on them both. As the day became night, Joe slept from time to time, drifting in and out as he held her hand.

Randy was making his way back to his small camp, hidden deep in the jungle. He was following a small river but was on the wrong side. He had found a place. The river got real shallow, and he could cross, only getting wet to his knees. It was a couple of miles beyond his camp and that made it a perfect place to cross. He had been incredibly careful in never following the same trail back to his camp, along with moving his base camp every week or so. In doing this, it made it nearly impossible for the cartel to track him. As he neared the river crossing, he heard voices. Freezing, he waited until he knew where they were. The voices seemed to be coming from in front and behind him. Quickly, he melted back into the jungle and disappeared from sight into the foliage. Quietly, he watched and listened. It was just a patrol, and they had no idea he was there. Not sure how many, Randy laid perfectly still and waited. As the two patrols met, they made a small camp and started cooking a meal. From his hiding spot, he watched, trying to figure out how many. He counted ten. Not sure what they were armed with, he didn't think it would be a good idea to get into a firefight.

After a few hours, the guys started settling down. It looked like they were going to stay all night. Carefully, Randy slid from his hiding spot. Taking out three grenades and quietly putting down his backpack, he slipped up a little closer. Pulling the pins from two, he tossed them into the center of the group of men. The pending explosion rocked the entire area as both grenades detonated simultaneously. Randy had ducked in behind a large tree and pulled the pin from the third grenade as he produced his silenced MP5, spraying death and destitution at anything that was still moving. Then he tossed in the last grenade. Retrieving his backpack, he crossed the river and started packing his camp. It was time to find a new hiding place.

Shortly after sunrise, Dr. Swenson walked in. Looking at Joe sleeping in the chair, he stood there.

Suddenly, Joe jerked wide awake. Looking around, he said, "Good morning, Doctor."

Then, reaching forward, he took Kay's hand and, standing up, he kissed her lightly on the forehead.

Looking from Joe to Kay and back, he said, "I have been talking to a surgeon in Seattle, and there was a procedure they, umm, *we* could do."

He explained to Joe that Kay had some bleeding inside her skull, causing pressure. They could drill a hole in her skull to relieve that pressure. He had never done it, but there were only two choices: do the procedure or remove her from life support and allow her to pass.

The tears started flowing as he thought about what Dr. Swenson had just said. Looking up at him, Joe said, "I'll have to call her family. I know this is my decision, but I have to tell her family. They are all supposed to be together today at her parents' house, and I'm gonna call shortly this afternoon. This is something we really need to talk about."

Joe sat holding Kay's hand and talking to her. From time to time, he would stand and lightly kiss her on the forehead. Pulling his chair closer, he stroked her hair and told her more about his time in Afghanistan and Colombia. Then he reached and picked up the phone and called.

Kay's oldest daughter, Alicia, answered on the second ring, saying, "Hi Joe, how are you doing? How are you holding up? How's Mom doing?" as she pushed the speaker button so everyone could hear and or ask questions.

Joe had to stop and settle down for a minute before he could begin.

"Hi everyone, I just had a conversation with the doctor. He's been talking to a surgeon in Seattle, and he thinks there is something they think they can do. I need everybody's advice before I can give my permission for them to do this." His voice broke, and he had to pause for a minute.

Starting over, he said, "The doctor here has never done this procedure, although the doctor in Seattle has and he says it's her only chance. They have to drill a small hole in her skull to relieve the pressure."

Pausing again for his voice to clear, he started again, "The weather is not supposed to change for a week or more. And as of now, they do not even see a break in the weather. There's no way to get her out or for somebody to get in. So now we have a big decision to make. All of you need to talk about this and tell me what you want me to do. I cannot make this decision alone."

They all said the same thing, "You're there, we are not. Do what you think is right. Although we are all in favor of trying this before taking her off life support."

Joe sat staring out the window and thinking. If he took her off life support, she would pass. If he let them operate, she could pass, anyway. He would not be responsible for letting her pass without the operation. Pushing the call button, he asked the nurse, "Is Dr. Swenson still here? The one that was in here talking to me a little while ago?"

Calling them back, Kay's mom, Sally answered, saying, "Hi Joe. I just want you to know we all love you."

Joe's eyes teared up again, and he had to take several breaths before he could continue.

Then, holding Kay's hand, he told them, "I'm going to sign the permission slip and have the operation done. I'll keep you all posted. But please, if there's a change of thoughts, let me know now."

He signed the release. The doctor called Seattle again, taking careful notes, and then they started to prepare Kay for surgery.

Joe sat there, staring at the wall, a total wreck. Waiting was the worst thing.

Two hours later, they brought Kay back to intensive care. She was still unconscious. They hooked her up to life support and waited.

Three days, they waited.

Joe never left her side. He was there twenty-four hours a day, talking to her, reading to her, anything that they thought would help. He was in contact with her family every day as well.

On the afternoon of the fourth day, after the procedure, Kay's parents and kids had decided if she didn't show signs of improvement in the next day or so, they should remove her from life support and allow her to pass.

Joe sat there next to Kay, holding her hand as he thought about the last several years. He thought about the first time he saw her; about slipping his number into her hand. Smiling, he thought about the afternoon he brought home their first side-by-side UTV. He told Kay, "Get ready but put on old clothes. We are going trail riding."

An hour into the ride, they came around a corner, and a huge water hole filled the trail. Laughing, he said, "You screamed but it was too late. I had already hit the gas. The water and mud flew, and we got absolutely drenched. When I looked over at you, well, the look on your face was priceless. Not to mention the water and mud dripping from both of us." Smiling, he looked down at her and continued, "All I could see was your eyes. They were coal black. I think you were mad at first. But I was laughing so hard. You finally broke and exploded into laughter."

Then he thought about the ski trip to Colorado when he asked her to marry him. Tears started as his memory continued with a million other thoughts as they raced through his mind. With tears running down both cheeks, he carefully reached down and tenderly kissed her on the forehead again.

Again, he thought about the first time he saw her, about their first words, about carrying her to their room, the night they got married. Carrying her off the mountain.

Could he have gotten her to the hospital faster? Should he have waited for the search party? As it was, he beat them up and back off the mountain. He took a deep breath and looked at Kay. Reaching down, he again gently kissed her. Then he laughed quietly. Looking at her, he asked, "Remember that night we went to supper then did a little bar hopping on the way back to town. You had to go to the bathroom, although we were miles from anyone or anywhere that had a bathroom. I stopped in the middle of the road, and you walked down into the ditch. Suddenly, I heard you scream and say, "Oh, yuck. Joe, get over here and help me." As I came around the end of the pickup you said, "Don't look!"

I asked, "How am I supposed to help if I can't look?" You said, "I don't know, just don't."

"I slowly walked around the pickup and there you were on all fours only backwards. With your pants around your knees, you were trying to keep your backside out of the swamp water in the ditch. I wanted to laugh so badly, but I knew better. That had to be one of the funniest things ever. I remember throwing my coat over your midsection as I walked into the water and helped you get to your feet. You have the cutest butt I've ever seen."

He was gently squeezing her hand, talking to her, and stroking her hair.

When Kay squeezed back, Joe froze.

Did I just imagine that? he wondered.

He called the nurse. As she came in, Joe told her what had just happened.

She said, "That can happen from time to time. It's a muscle reaction to what you we're doing."

As she took Kay's vitals, he squeezed again, although he had stopped stroking her hair. Again, he gently squeezed her hand.

Again, she squeezed back.

Only this time, her eyes started to flutter and open. Joe's eyes filled with tears as he looked from his wife to the nurse and back. Joe reached down, gently kissed his wife, and said, "Oh, thank you, God. I love you, Kay. I love you so much." Then, looking up, he quietly mouthed, "Thank you."

Kay whispered, "I love you too," as she gave him a weak smile.

Joe said, "I once made you a promise, do you remember? I said that I would always protect you." She smiled again and said, "I know, and you always will."

Part Two

Chapter Twelve

Joe arrived home after a month-long chase involving a very large and very cantankerous old male polar bear. The bear refused to fall for any of the traps Joe had set up. The one time he did go in a trap, he just tore it apart and got out, sending him back to the drawing board.

He was trying to design and build a trap that could hold a fifteen hundred pound mad bear. What he had to work with was very limited, but Joe finally found everything he needed. In a matter of a few days, he had a better and much stronger trap built.

He could have tranquilized the bear, although a tranquilizer was very dangerous. The amount used depended on the weight of the target. Not enough, and the bear wakes up early and in a terrible mood. Too much, and he would have a dead bear on his hands.

Joe guaranteed his work and was paid to do what the customer wanted. The Canadian government wanted the bear relocated. The only way he would get paid is if the bear died of self-defense, and someone had better be bleeding before the bear.

The third week, while out looking for the bear, he found a dead seal on the ice. It was only about half-gone. He used it for bait, and it worked. Polar bears live mostly on seals. With the dead seal and his new trap, two days later, he had captured a real grouchy bear.

Getting the trap off the ice was another story, but with winches and come-alongs, some chains, and a couple of snowmobiles, it finally came off. They got it loaded on a type of sled trailer and hooked behind a snowcat, and off they went.

They took the bear about a hundred miles to the east and released it. As they opened the trap, all it wanted to do was kill everyone and everything in the area. It attacked the sled, then the snowcat, trying to get inside and at the people.

Joe thought he was going to have to shoot it. Although, after an angry session, it finally wandered off.

They had a two-day trip back to the village. Where Joe contacted a bush pilot and started his trip home the following day. He could hardly wait to see Kay.

He called her as soon as he landed in Whitehorse Yukon. That was the first time he had talked to her in over a month.

He said, "I'll see you tomorrow afternoon."

Kay's voice started to break up. He knew she was crying. He really missed her, also. After her ordeal in Alaska, they spent the next six weeks together.

Joe had helped her with all the physical therapy. He also attended to all of her personal needs. He wouldn't let the hospital staff anywhere close to her. If she needed anything, by God, she got it.

This was the first time they had been apart.

Joe's trip home was anything but simple. He had flown in a bush plane to Whitehorse, Yukon, commercial to Anchorage, Alaska, then to Seattle, Washington, and from there, he would head to Minneapolis, Minnesota, and on to Chicago.

Kay picked him up at Midway Airport. Joe hated flying into Chicago O'Hare. Way too big and busy. You could get lost there for a week, he would say. It's easier to find your way out of the mountains and less dangerous.

They stopped for dinner on their way home, but Joe just wanted to get home and spend a quiet evening with Kay.

Arriving home, he hauled in the supplies. The rest would arrive in a few days. Taking a quick shower, he built a fire while Kay got a couple of bottles of beer.

Together, they sat on the couch and talked for several hours. Then she started talking about taking a vacation. Joe sensed she was up to something and figured they were going to someplace like New York City.

He just sat and listened, and when she said Montana, he started smiling. *All right,* he thought, *time with Kay alone, in the mountains. This time, I'll be with her from here to there and back.*

As they talked and started planning their trip to Montana, Joe said, "I'll start packing everything we need tomorrow. Let's take our plane and make a few stops along the way. Say like, maybe Iowa. I believe you have a few family members living there and a couple of grandkids."

Kay started smiling at the mention of grandkids and said, "Wow, really? Can we stop and see my daughters and the grandkids?"

Joe replied, "I don't see why not. We are on a vacation, right?"

She couldn't stop smiling and said, "That would be great. How long do you think we will be gone? I have about four weeks of vacation time coming, and I can take more."

Joe thought about it and said, "That should be more than enough." Checking to make sure the doors were locked. He took her hand and together, they walked towards their bedroom.

Joe had a restless night full of dreams and nightmares. Again, he was dreaming about his past. A past that would never leave him alone. A past that would continue to haunt his nights.

Randy had sat on the hillside overlooking the compound for several hours and watched as people passed through. As he watched, he thought, *Those guards at the gate must know everyone by sight.* Then he watched as he noticed a large truck

heading towards the gate. Picking up his binoculars, he watched as the truck stopped. One guard walked around and glanced at the back. Randy saw his chance, thinking,

This is too good to pass. Picking up his equipment, he headed back to his makeshift camp.

Before the sun rose, Randy was up and quickly made a small fire and coffee as he started putting what he needed into a backpack.

Then, heading off through the jungle, he followed the road but stayed out of sight. Thinking he was about ten miles or so from the compound, he went to work.

An hour later, he heard the truck coming. He knew the truck would have to slow its way down as it crossed the bridge. Randy worked his way to the bridge and, as the truck was making the turn, he ran out behind and jumped into the back.

Carefully, he placed the bomb and then tossed all the evidence he had stolen to make it look like another cartel.

This should cause one hell of a shit storm.

He slipped out of the truck and ran for the cover of the jungle.

Making his way through the jungle, he was about a mile away when he heard the bomb go off. If everything went as planned, it should have gone off shortly after the truck was parked for the night. Hopefully, in the loading dock and just before the loading had begun for the following day's delivery.

Arriving at his hiding spot high on the hillside, he watched the chaos the explosion caused. Two buildings were on fire, and there were people running everywhere.

Laying on his stomach with his sniper rifle in position, he scanned the area for the people he was sent to kill. After an hour, only one of the cartel's upper echelons had shown up. With the fire blazing, the entire area was lit up.

Randy spotted his target for the second time. This time, he followed the guy until he stopped in the middle of the compound, shouting orders and pointing his arms.

Randy's finger crawled to the trigger as his eye moved from the spotting scope to the rifle scope. Putting the crosshairs on the center of his ear, he slowly squeezed the trigger.

The bullet found its mark and Geraldo Garcia was knocked sideways into the path of an oncoming truck. The driver stood on the brake pedal, but it was too late. The truck hit him, running over his head, making him impossible to identify and covering the fact that he had been shot.

Under the cover of darkness, he quickly packed up his equipment. Then thought about where to head next to cause more hate and discontent between the cartels.

The next morning, Joe woke in a cold sweat. Carefully, he looked around before moving. Then, slowly, he got up.

He was making coffee as Kay came walking into the kitchen. He handed her a cup. "I'll start packing and get ready to go. If everything goes right, we should be able to leave later today or tomorrow."

He then kissed Kay as she headed to the office to tell her

boss she would be gone for a month and finish up a few loose ends.

By three that afternoon, she was heading home.

They finished loading the plane that night, went home, and enjoyed another quiet evening in front of the fireplace.

By noon the next day, they were cleared for takeoff as their twin-engine Cessna 310 went wheels up, turned to the west and headed for Iowa. They wanted to spend a couple of days with friends and family in Iowa before going wheels up for Montana.

Just two hours after taking off from Midway Airport, Joe turned the Cessna 310 from base to final at the Shenandoah County Airport in Shenandoah, Iowa. Reaching over, he nudged Kay a few times to wake her up.

Rubbing her eyes, she asked, "Where are we?"

As they turned, Kay glanced at the terminal and said with a smile, "Those people standing there look very familiar."

Joe glanced at the terminal, then back at the runway as he replied, "They should, it's your family."

Kay looked at Joe and said, "How did they know? I never said anything when I talked to them yesterday. I wasn't sure we were stopping."

Joe smiled as the plane touched down. "I called them after you fell asleep and told them we would be there in about an hour."

Kay reached over and kissed his cheeks. "Thank you,

honey. You really are a sweet guy."

Joe started to laugh. "Wow, don't tell anyone else that. I don't want it to get out. Most of my friends think I'm a hard ass."

Spending time with Kay's family was everything Joe expected and more. Joe got along with Kay's kids and the grandkids were calling him Grandpa Joe in a few days.

After a three-day visit, it was time to head west again. Joe knew he wanted to stop at Logan's, although there might not be time. He also wanted to spend some time with a friend in the Flathead Valley before they headed into the Bob Marshal Wilderness area of northwestern Montana for a couple of weeks of alone time with Kay.

The flight to Rapid City was smooth. Stopping, they gassed up again, had lunch and headed for Sheridan, Wyoming, landing just before dark. They got a room in Sheridan, Wyoming and spent the night.

Joe then looked at the air charts to see how he wanted to cross over the divide. Walking back to the lobby, Joe made a couple of cups of tea. Entering their room, he handed one to a smiling Kay. Kissing her, they walked over and sat down to enjoy a movie before they headed for bed.

Joe woke just as the movie ended. Looking over at Kay, he took the empty teacup out of her hand. Then, slowly, he tried to stand without waking her.

Just as he started walking towards the bathroom, she

asked, "Is the movie over? Did I sleep through the whole thing? How did it end?"

Joe replied, "I have no idea. We both slept through the movie. Although I stayed awake long enough to put my cup down." He held up her empty cup.

Standing, she started getting ready for bed. Joe walked out of the bathroom to see his wife standing in a sheer black nightie. Stopping, he let his eyes work their way up and down. Shaking his head, he said, "Just when I think you couldn't get any more beautiful, you prove me wrong." Taking her hand, he slowly pulled her on top. He laid back onto the bed as he slid his arms around her and rolled her onto her back.

Joe tossed and turned all night. Several times, Kay had awakened to try to comfort him.

He was in Afghanistan. He had heard of a valley high in the mountains that had a bumper crop of poppies. He wanted desperately to find that valley. The heroin they made was sent to the US and was the cash crop the Taliban used to purchase guns, ammunition, and bomb-making supplies.

Randy was several hundred feet behind a small group of men making their way up a trail that was barely visible. He was sure this group would lead him to the valley. Once he was sure they had a destination in mind, he broke off and climbed above them. That way, he could see where they were headed and if there were more waiting.

Randy followed until they arrived at the valley. He didn't want to kill any of these guys. From what he could tell, they were being forced to harvest the poppies. From high above, he watched as the men went to work gathering and filling sacks. He had ten incendiary bombs with him and planned on destroying the field later that night. The field looked to be about five acres. He also had several pounds of Semtex plastic explosives, and a military version of C4. Hopefully, enough to close the trail between the two mountains. Or at least make it hard to access. He wanted the Taliban to get careless in hunting him. Mad people make bad decisions and stupid mistakes. That way, he hoped he could eliminate as many as possible.

With the men gone, it was time for him to work. Carefully, he made his way into the small valley. Planting all ten of the bombs, he was quite sure it would completely destroy the crop. Then, finding the narrowest point between the two mountains, he planted the C4. He wanted the bombs to bring down as much rock as possible. He set them to go off a few seconds apart as they climbed the mountainside.

It worked just like he wanted. It would be nearly impossible for anyone to clear the rock away and get into the valley from this direction again.

Joe woke to the sound of running water. Rolling over, he saw Kay's nightie where he had thrown it the night before. Picking it up, he said, "This did what it is designed to do. Only stay on for a few minutes." Laughing, he placed it on Kay's suitcase and walked into the bathroom. Kay was standing there, wrapped only in a towel, as he put his arms around her from behind.

Kay turned in his arms and, wrapping hers around him, she said, "Didn't you get enough, last night?" She met his lips.

Joe kissed her lips and slid down her neck, kissing as he moved and replied, "Oh you, my beautiful lady, I'll never get enough." Taking a hold of the towel, he led her out of the bathroom and back to bed.

A couple of hours later, they arrived back at the airport. Joe started going over the plane. He always did a very thorough preflight inspection. Although this time, he spent more time looking things over. Kay noticed and asked, "You always do a complete preflight. Although today, you're checking everything closer and twice. Did you notice or feel something coming in yesterday?"

He replied, "Nope, not at all, although we will be flying over some really tall and rugged mountains today. It's some of the roughest countries in Montana. I don't want any problems. Besides, I think we might make another stop. Logan lives just an hour or so flight time from here. I'm going to call him en route and see if he's mowed the grass on the runway lately."

Joe filed an IFR flight plan for Logan's ranch. Although, he was intending to fly by visual flight rules. He had an instrument rating and figured anything short of a thunderstorm, he would just fly through.

As they went wheels up and left Sheridan, Wyoming, he called Logan. Logan answered, saying, "Hey buddy, where are you?"

Joe replied, "Passing through zero nine thousand headed for one five thousand and about one hundred fifty miles east of you."

Logan paused for a couple of seconds. "So you're in the Sheridan area, right?"

Joe chuckled. "Yeah, we just left Sheridan."

"Now, wouldn't that have been easier than all this pilot talk?"

Joe glanced at the instruments. "Maybe, but it's too much fun to mess with you and make you think. Hey, have you cut the grass on the runway lately?"

"No, I haven't. How long do I have before you get here?"

"We are about an hour or so out."

Logan swore under his breath. "I'll have it done before you get here."

"That sounds great. I'll pull the power back a little and give you a little extra time. See you in say, just over an hour or so."

"That sounds fantastic. See you shortly," replied Logan as he ended the call.

A little over an hour later, Joe made a pass over Logan's Rocking L ranch. Seeing the runway all mowed, he looked at the windsock and set up to land. Taxiing to the tie down area, he pulled the throttles to an idle and shut down both engines. As they exited the plane, Logan was standing there.

Grabbing Joe in a bear hug, the two men shook hands. Turning, Logan pulled Kay into a hug, saying, "God, I miss you two. How are you feeling? I couldn't believe it when Joe called me from Alaska and told me what had happened. That man is the only one I know who could do something like that. I can't believe how calm he stays when everything turns to shit."

Kay glanced at her husband. "You don't have to tell me that. He is one amazing guy. Don't tell him I said that."

They were both laughing as Joe walked up to them after tying the plane down and said, "What did I miss? Are you two plotting against me?"

Logan continued laughing. "Nothing like that. I was trying to get this beautiful lady to run off with me."

Joe grabbed Logan in another hug. "Sorry, buddy, she's taken. You'll have to find another."

Logan slapped Joe on the back and said, "Come on. I think I have a couple of cold beers in the fridge. You are staying the night?"

Looking at Kay, Joe asked, "Are we?"

Kay replied, "Don't put this on me. I'm on vacation, remember?"

Logan said, "It's settled then. Grab whatever you need,

and we'll head for the house."

Logan took Joe and Kay upstairs to his private domain. After showing them where they would be sleeping, he said, "I'll see you two downstairs shortly. I'll show you around the ranch."

A few minutes later, the three of them left the house and started walking towards the barns when a black and white painted colt came running up. Logan wrapped his arms around the young stallion and said, "CJ get out of here. You damn pest."

Kay asked, "Where on earth did you find him? My God, He is beautiful. I absolutely love his markings."

Logan replied, "I got him a few weeks ago. I was looking for some new breeding stock, and the lady I was dealing with had him. He ran right up to me and stuck his nose under my arm. I couldn't resist. Besides, he's just so damn cute.

"His mother comes from a long line of some of the best cow horses in Montana. Although, I think his dad is a sneaky mustang stud from a herd just south of here. I'm sure he jumped the fence and spent a romantic night with her before leaving in the morning and returning to his herd before anyone saw him.

"With that breeding, I'm sure he'll make one heck of a cow horse. He's so smart and learns quickly. In the first couple of days here, he figured out how to open the gates and get out all the time. Got to be a real nuisance. I must have put him back in his stall twenty times. I finally gave up when I figured out he just wanted to follow me around. He now has the run of the ranch.

"He absolutely torments some of the guys and talks about getting into trouble. Every day someone yells at him. He just prances off with his head and tail up as if to say, you can't catch me. Although you can try."

They stand there watching as the colt walked over and noses a water bucket. Not wanting a drink, he tipped it over and walked away.

Logan said, "See what I mean? He's just a little pain. But I sure do love him."

As they walked around looking at the cattle and horses, CJ followed along constantly, sticking his nose into everything. When one of the hands yelled at him, he would toss his head and prance off. Although he never let Logan get very far away or out of his sight. Several times, he came up to get scratched or petted. They spent an hour walking around and then headed for the house.

With supper waiting on the table, they sat down to eat. After supper, they then headed back upstairs. The rest of the evening, they relaxed, enjoyed a couple of beers and conversation. Logan asked questions about Alaska and what had happened.

Joe started by telling him about the time they spent camping and hiking. About the weather the day Kay left.

About the hole they had tried to get through. Then about his climb to where the plane lay bent and twisted beyond recognition. About the trip back down and killing that huge old bear. As he talked, Kay's eyes got bigger and bigger. She had been unconscious during most of the trip down the mountain and knew very little about it, other than what some of the hospital staff had told her and a few people from the town.

Joe said, "I need to use the restroom."

Logan replied, "There's one down that hall, second door on the right."

Watching as Joe walked away, he turned to Kay and said, "He is definitely one in a thousand, maybe one in a million."

Kay smiled and replied, "More like one in ten million."

Logan nodded his head. "If someone would have told me what he just did, I would have been tempted to call him a liar. Although not Joe. I've hunted with him. He is definitely one in a million and probably the best friend I have. He called me and asked if something happened, and he didn't call me back for a few days. Well, he asked me to come to find the two of you and take care of things. He knew he was up against it. After listening to what he said just now, along with the fact I'm sure he left most of it out. Anyway, there's a valley west of here just over those mountains"—he pointed out the window. Kay turned her head to look—"Joe saw that valley and told me he wanted to be buried up there and if the worst happened, you with him."

Kay's eyes filled with tears as Logan talked about Joe. Logan knew a few things that no one else knew, and without divulging anything, Logan said, "What he did isn't impossible. It's called love. It's the love he has for you, along with what he loves to do. Go one on one with nature. He comes out on top all the time. I've spent many hours with him in the woods and on the phone. I can tell what you mean to him without him saying it. It's the way he talks that says more than the words. It's the look in his eyes and the way he moves. He's always placing himself between you and any type of possible danger. Watch him tomorrow if you don't believe me. You'll see. Believe me, you'll see. Once you know what you're looking at or for."

Joe walked back into the upstairs sitting area with three more beers. Opening them, he handed one to each. Taking the third with him, he said, "To the best of friends we will always be. Today, tomorrow, for eternity." Bumping bottles with Logan, he continued, "Life and love had passed me by. Until the day I caught your eye. A friendship and a marriage that will always last. Live for today and forget the past." Bumping bottles with Kay, he took a drink as he sat down next to her.

Looking from Kay to Logan and back, he asked, "Did I miss something?"

Logan replied, "Nope, just the fact you are one amazing friend and I'm glad you're my friend."

Kay added, "And husband, don't forget that. And I'm with Logan. I'm so glad you're my husband." Reaching over, she gave Joe a kiss and said, "I'm headed for bed. I need my beauty sleep."

Logan and Joe both stood as Kay got up and walked away.

Watching, Logan said, "I think she could stay awake for the rest of her life, and she'd still be gorgeous."

"Yeah, I'm with you on that. She is definitely very easy on the eyes."

Logan replied, "Hear, hear," as he bumped Joe's bottle. Getting up, he said, "One more or bedtime."

The two friends talked for a few more minutes and headed off to bed. Joe tossed and turned all night. Several times, Kay woke to sounds of him talking or making different noises she couldn't explain.

Randy had spent all night running, and they were still on his trail. He had used every trick he knew and could not shake them. He was only a few miles from Bogota, and they stuck to him like glue.

He approached the town, and he started looking for the American flag. Bogota was bigger than he thought, and he was not sure where the American embassy was. He had destroyed all his equipment, at least made it unusable by anyone. He had also set several traps in his camp when they found it. Well, it would be the last thing they would ever find. Plugging the barrel on his sniper rifle, he was sure they would backfire and either kill whoever shot them or at least severely injure them. Now armed only with his MP5, two pistols, and a knife, he walked through the city. A couple of times, he had asked where the American embassy was, only to have the people he asked walk off. He was sure the cartel had put the word out that if anyone helped a gringo stranger, they would suffer.

As he walked, he watched alleys and buildings for signs he had been found. Looking at the street signs, he worked his way towards the city center. He was sure the embassy would be near other government buildings. He turned a corner and watched as a guy walked in his direction. The MP5 hung from a sling and was under a light jacket. He had a knife in his left hand and pressed up against his arm. His Kimber .45 was in a shoulder holster while the H and K .45 were in a holster at the small of his back where his right hand could easily get to it.

As the man got close, Randy watched as his right hand came up with a pistol. His left arm had flashed and suddenly, a knife appeared protruding from the man's chest. Randy stopped, pulling the knife, he looked around. He watched as two more guys approached. Kicking one in the chest, he slipped the knife under the second one's chin and asked in Spanish, "Where is the US embassy?"

As the first guy started getting up, Randy kicked him again in the side of the head. The guy's eyes rolled up, and down he went.

Looking at the other, he asked again, "Where is the US embassy?"

The man looked at him and spat in his face. Randy pushed the knife up about a half inch into his throat and asked again. The guy's eyes were huge as he grabbed at his throat. Randy said, "That won't kill you, although you have one more chance, or I'll push it the rest of the way." The man pointed, and Randy pulled the knife down and drove his fist into the guy's forehead, watching as the man crumpled into a pile on the ground.

Randy took off at a run, with only three blocks to go, he would be safe. Rounding the last corner, he saw several guys standing in the street.

Opening his coat, he brought the MP5 into firing position as he continued to walk toward them. With the stock extended, he took aim and waited. With his only eyes moving, he continued to walk. He heard a guy say stop, or we'll shoot. Randy touched the trigger and three bullets spat from the barrel, showing three red spots on the guy's chest. Just then, everything turned to shit.

With bullets flying, Randy dropped to the ground and started shooting. A few seconds later, he was up and sprinting towards the embassy gate and safety.

A squad of marines stood ready just inside the gate, waiting to defend the embassy and any US citizens. He could see the gates opening and the marines on the other side waiting to return fire until they were fired upon. As Randy ran past the gate to safety, they opened up, sending all the pursuers running for cover while a few just dropped. They would never run or kill again.

Just inside the gate, Randy fell to the ground. He had been hit five times: Twice in his left leg, once in his right with one more high in his chest, plus one in his back.

Joe woke, grabbing his chest. He slipped from the bedroom and down the hall. Opening the door, he walked out onto the deck and stared into the night sky. Slowly, his breathing started to level out, and he began to calm down. Looking at his legs, he could see the marks where the bullets had torn into his flesh that December day so long ago. Pausing for several minutes, he finally turned and walked back to the bedroom. He grabbed his jeans, then went downstairs to make coffee.

A few minutes later, Logan walked in and poured a cup. They sat there talking about the ranch as Logan got up and got out a frying pan and bacon. A few minutes later, Kay came walking in. Sitting next to Joe, Logan handed her a cup and said, "Good morning, sunshine."

Kay looked at him and said, "Sunshine. What are you talking about? The birds aren't even up yet."

Logan looked at Joe and said, "Not a morning person?"

Joe just smiled as he filled her cup again. Looking at

Logan, he said, "At least one full pot, with a strong possibility of two."

Logan chuckled as he turned and started frying eggs. Turning the pan-fried potatoes, he asked, "How do you like your eggs?"

Joe replied, "Surprise us. However you cook them will work. We are not too picky, and she won't notice for another hour. By then, it's too late."

Kay stretched and let out a huge yawn. Looking from Joe to Logan and back, she said, "I'm awake," as she yawned again.

Joe smiled as Logan started to laugh.

Kay said, "It's not fair to pick on me before I'm able to defend myself."

Joe reached over and kissed her on the forehead, saying, "We are not picking on you. It's just you're so cute when you first wake up. You walk around in a daze for at least an hour."

"I'm not in a daze. I know where we are and where we are going."

"Okay then, where are we?"

Kay smiled. "Logan's ranch. The Rocking L, in umm, Wyoming."

Joe looked at Logan and said, "Well, she's half right. We are at your ranch, and it is the Rocking L." He filled her cup for the fourth time.

Logan snickered as he said, "Well, if we were about forty

miles south, we would be in Wyoming."

Everyone turned and looked out the window as they heard *clomp, clomp, clomp* on the front deck. Suddenly, a black head with a white blaze appeared in the window. Logan walked to the door. Opening it, CJ tried to walk into the kitchen only to have Logan stop him and start pushing him backwards, saying, "CJ, you damn pest. Get out of here. Go away for God's sake. Go bother someone else for a while." Pushing the young colt back onto the deck, Logan followed him out and stood staring at the distant mountains. CJ, seeing the door open, headed towards it. Kay had just picked up her cup as CJ walked through the door and stuck his nose against her cheek. Kay screamed. Dropping her cup, she jumped to her feet and started walking backwards, tripping over the chair, she fell backwards to the floor.

Both Joe and Logan came running to see what was happening. Just as CJ put his head down by her like he was checking to make sure she was okay. Logan, grabbing his halter, pulled his head up and led him out of the house. Joe reached down and helped Kay to her feet, asking, "Are you alright?"

Kay replied, "Yeah, umm, yeah. Yes, and ummm, I'm also wide awake. Who, why, what? What the hell is a horse doing in the house?"

Logan walked back in saying, "That's just CJ. He thinks it's okay for him to go or be anywhere I am and sometimes he's a real pest."

Joe just stood back and snickered as his big city wife was introduced to the wilds of Montana. Although it was 2020, Logan's life was more like the 1880s. He lived the rancher's life where everything he did was around animals, either horses or cattle.

Logan's ranch, the Rocking L, is over 75,000 acres. He's a fourth-generation rancher and inherited the ranch when he was only 17, when his parents were killed in a plane crash coming home from a meeting in Helena.

His paternal great great great grandparents settled in the valley in the late 1860s. They had been with a wagon train headed west when they stopped in what is now Billings, Montana. His ancestors had heard of a valley to the south. Hiring a trapper, they had departed the wagon train in search of the hidden valley beyond what is now the Bear Tooth mountains of south-central Montana. Seeing the valley from high in the mountains, the Lathrop family decided this was where they were going to settle, thus starting the Rocking L.

After spending a few days on the Rocking L, Joe and Kay decided it was time to continue their vacation.

Getting the plane loaded and ready to go, Joe filed a fight plan and prepared to depart this beautiful area of Montana. Kay stood next to the plane, looking at the mountains and petting CJ, who had become her best friend, after scaring her half to death just a couple of days earlier.

Joe and Logan talked about the possibility of a hunting trip the following year. Saying goodbye, Logan shook Joe's hand and gave Kay a hug. Taking CJ by the halter, he led the young stallion away from the plane and runway as Joe throttled up the twin engine Cessna and taxied down to prepare for takeoff. Lining up in the center of the runway, Joe pushed the throttles and props forward. As the plane gained speed and rotated, Joe contacted Billings' air traffic control. Opening the flight plan, he banked left and headed to the west. As they climbed through zero seven thousand and headed for zero eight thousand, they approached the continental divide. The left engine started missing. Joe quickly applied the intake heat, and just a few minutes later, the engine quit.

Kay asked, "Oh my God, Joe. What's happening?"

Joe put his finger up to his lips as he called out, "Mayday, mayday. This is Cessna Papa Romeo 3469. We have engine failure. We are about eighty miles east of Butte, Montana, on a vector of 285 degrees at 7,500 feet. I cannot get the plane to climb. Mayday, mayday. I repeat, Cessna Papa Romeo 3469 inbound Butte, Montana. We have a dead engine and losing altitude!"

As Joe talked on the radio, calling out his problem, he feathered the prop all the way. Shutting off the intake heat and playing with the throttle, he finally got the Cessna to climb. They crossed over the divide with only a couple hundred feet to spare and started their descent to Butte airport, where they were cleared to land, still under emergency conditions.

Joe landed short, exiting the runway at the second taxiway. Taxiing right up to the shop, killing the engine, he exited the aircraft and walked into the shop. He talked to the mechanic, telling him what the plane had done.

Lee, the shop foreman, listened and said, "Sounds like a fuel pump problem."

Three hours later, with not one but two new fuel pumps, they lifted off for Kalispell, Montana, where they planned on staying with friends for a couple of days before continuing their vacation in the Bob Marshal Wilderness Area.

While visiting with friends, they went to get everything arranged and started packing what they would take with them into the Bob Marshall Wilderness area of Northwest Montana.

Chapter Thirteen

As Joe was packing things and loading the horses, he thought,

Wow! Two weeks with Kay alone.

He looked over at her.

She was looking at him, and they were both smiling.

Everything was packed, but before they mounted up and headed to the wilderness area, Joe got out the guns they would carry. Kay had a .357 Magnum loaded with 158-grain brass jacketed hollow points. He knew it was a lot of gun for her but was confident that, if needed, she could handle it. She would also have a Winchester model '94 in .375 caliber loaded with 220-grain hollow points. Joe had his .44 Magnum loaded with 200-grain hollow points. He also carried a Henry lever action in .45–70 loaded with 500-grain solid core. Getting hit by that would be like getting hit by a lead pumpkin.

Kay had been in grizzly country many times before, nevertheless, Joe gave her a refresher course as they rode along. "Watch, listen, and always have one of your guns with you. Besides grizzlies, there are black bears, wolverines, wolves, and mountain lions. Any one of those can give you trouble and wreck your day."

Kay smiled at him and said, "Do we have to think we'll have any trouble?"

Joe looked at the surrounding mountains and said, "Probably not, although we should always be ready. You just never know."

Kay had her camera out and was taking pictures as they rode through this heaven on earth area. Almost 1,600 square miles of untouched beauty. There were very few roads inside the wilderness area other than a few forest service roads. They mostly followed game trails.

Joe and Kay had picked a high mountain lake to set up their base camp. It was a long three- or four-day ride, although the beautiful scenery and the wildlife made up for long days in the saddle.

Each afternoon, they would stop a couple of hours before dark and set up camp. Joe would unsaddle the horses and the packhorses, water, and feed them, and then picket them. They slept in a small two-person tent, two sleeping bags and a campfire made their camp. Kay would cook their dinner on a small camp stove, and after that, they would clean everything up.

No food scraps left lying around. After all, they were in bear country. Then they would sit around the fire, drinking tea and making their plans for the next day. As they crawled to their sleeping bags, they would place each pistol on a white towel. If they had unwanted company at night, that would make finding them much easier.

One more check of the camp and they crawled into their

sleeping bags. Joe reached over, pulling Kay just a little closer. Kissing her, he said, "So what do you think so far? Are you having a good time?"

Kay wrapped her arms around him as she replied, "Logan's an absolute hoot. And CJ, he's amazing. My God, he's beautiful. So other than the problem with the plane, everything has been just fantastic."

Joe yawned. "I'm sure most of our troubles are over and we are going to have a fantastic time." Then, he drifted off to sleep.

Early in the morning, Joe started to thrash around.

Kay woke and listened to what he was saying, trying to figure out what was bothering him and causing these terrible nightmares.

He was hanging from a chain in the ceiling. His hands were tied, and his feet were off the ground. A man walked up behind him and slashed a razor-sharp knife across his back. Randy gritted his teeth to not cry out and give these drug pushing pricks the satisfaction they were looking for.

He continued to thrash and moan, but never said one word that could be understood.

In the morning, they would get the coffee going, then sit and watch as the mountains came to life when Kay asked, "Joe, what are you dreaming about? They seem to really bother you. You thrash around and mumble but very seldom say anything that I can understand. You had a terrible nightmare last night. I sat next to you and held your hand."

Joe looked at her and lied, "I have no idea. I don't remember anything. I'm sorry if I kept you awake."

Kay took a sip of her coffee, staring at the mountains for a minute. She turned to Joe, looked him in the eyes and said, "That wasn't the first time. It's happened many times." Then, reaching over, she cupped his cheek. "You don't have to tell until you want to. I'll just always do my best to comfort you."

Joe looked at her, saying, "Thanks, maybe someday. Let's get breakfast started."

After breakfast, Joe got the horses ready while Kay repacked what they had used and made sure the fire was completely out. After checking everything again, they mounted up for that day's ride.

Sometimes, they would stop earlier in the day by a creek or small lake and give the horses some extra rest and go swimming and/or fishing.

A nice swim was always refreshing, although the water was starting to cool off. The fishing was fantastic, and fresh fish for supper was always a treat after long hours in the saddle.

After four days of riding, they made the high mountain lake where Kay had wanted to set up their base camp. From here, they could ride in any direction they wanted to sightsee and take pictures, fish, or just relax in a high mountain meadow. The fall colors were starting, and the scenery was absolutely beautiful.

One evening, Kay spotted some mountain goats up high on a jagged cliff, and they decided to try to get closer in the morning. Kay wanted to get some pictures for the magazine. They started climbing at sunrise. Through binoculars, they could see them several hundred feet above. But it took five hours to get above them. They slowly looked over the edge, and the goats were just a hundred feet away, looking downhill. Kay took several pictures of the two billies, four nannies, and several kits. They spent two hours watching the kits as the sure-footed little rascals could run and jump or just stand on ledges too narrow for a person to hang onto, let alone walk.

They were truly something spectacular to sit and watch. On the way down, Joe stopped short. He had seen something, but what? They slowly peeked over the ledge, and a mother mountain lion with three six-month-old cubs were on the hunt. Kay took several more pictures before the wind changed and the scent spooked the cats and they disappeared.

Just before dark, they were back in camp. What a day! They were both exhausted. Kay made a light supper while Joe checked and took care of the horses. Like always, they cleaned the camp spotless, had tea, talked, and headed for their sleeping bags, making sure to place those two pistols where they could be found quickly if needed.

Randy walked into fire base Delta and asked for the

camp's commanding officer. Commander Isaac Mason walked in a few minutes later. Sticking out his hand, he said, "I'm the camp Commander."

Taking the hand, Randy said, "I'm commander Randal Jackson, call sign Ghost."

Isaac stepped back and saluted Randy and replied, "Anything you need, just ask."

Randy sat down and simply said, "I'm done. I want to go home."

After four years, six months, and eleven days, Randy wanted out and just wanted to go home. He had 358 confirmed kills. He was the most hated and wanted man in Afghanistan. The Taliban had a price on his head.

Six days later, he was standing in front of the pentagon awaiting his discharge papers. Because of his assignment, his papers had to come from the top. He spent two weeks being debriefed before his discharge was approved.

The next morning, while eating breakfast, they heard a loud crash. Kay jumped up, looking around. Joe just sat there and laughed. It was September, and the bighorn sheep were just starting to rut. When two big males collided, it could be heard a mile away.

Joe quickly started saddling the horses while Kay got things cleaned up and put away. She did one more quick check-over and double-checked to make sure the fire was out. Then they swung up in the saddle and headed toward the sound of the battle.

As they were riding, they could still hear the crashes. They sounded like they were right over the hill. They dismounted and ground tied the horses and very carefully walked up the hill.

Nothing.

The crashing rams were further away.

Walking back down, they mounted and kept following the sound. They topped a hill and Joe pointed and said, "There they are. Look. There are five, no, six."

It was remarkable. The sheep were so busy butting heads they did not pay any attention to the two horses at all. Kay continued to snap pictures. They stayed on the horses and watched. It was absolutely unbelievable.

Joe explained, "When males come together during mating season, they fight for the right to breed. Usually, during this time of year, they get a little stupid and you can walk up on them at times. During the rest of the year, they are very hard to find, and are very shy, and will disappear in a hurry."

Kay replied, "Oh, so they get like most males when they get horny."

Joe started laughing and replied, "Aww yes," as he pulled his hat down and backed his horse away and turned, heading down the trail. Stopping at a better viewpoint, they sat there watching the bighorns. Kay took out her binoculars and looked at the side of the hill to her left. Joe looked at Kay, waiting to hear what she was looking at.

She asked, "What is that over there, about halfway up the hill?"

Joe had to back his horse up to see. As he looked, it turned and faced him. The light reflected off his huge palmated antlers.

"That's a huge bull moose standing about a mile away in a meadow," Joe replied. "Want to get a closer look?"

Looking at the bighorns one more time, Kay said, "Absolutely, that sounds great."

They rode across the valley and started heading up the hill when a pack of wolves trotted out of the woods and headed for the bull. He slowly picked up his head and turned their way. They stopped about two hundred yards away, waiting to see what would happen next. This was nature at its fullest. Only the strongest would survive.

The big bull watched the wolves but made no attempt to run. One wolf turned and headed toward the bull. He lowered his head and put his huge antlers towards the wolf. The wolf just turned and kept trotting along.

Joe looked at Kay and said, "That pack may have killed that moose. Although as big as he is, one or more wolves would have been injured or killed in the fight. That pack is small, and every wolf there is needed to ensure their survival."

They continued watching the wolves and the moose. No

more attempts were made to chase the moose. They just kept moving, looking for easier prey. The moose just went on grazing on the grass and brush in the area.

The afternoon was warm and enjoyable. They rode, talked, and pointed at different things they saw. They topped a large hill and looked back. The valley spread out behind them. The sight was nothing short of spectacular. Kay looked around and said, "Oh my God, what I wouldn't give to stay here with you for the rest of my life!"

Joe looked at his wife and agreed, saying, "I could think of nothing better."

Kay looked at her watch. "We had better head back. It's getting late."

As they rode back, Joe reached and took Kay's hand. They rode back in silence, just holding hands and looking around. Every time they looked at each other, they both smiled. The love between them was unbelievable. Kay thought she was the luckiest girl in the world. Although Joe knew he was the luckiest guy.

Back at camp, the routine was the same. Joe took care of the horses, and Kay started supper. As Joe walked back from where the horses were, Kay was busy and did not hear him walk up.

Joe slipped up behind her, reached around, and slowly turned Kay around. Taking her in his arms, he gently kissed her. She responded like a woman in love. The two stood there, slowly dancing to an unheard song. As far as they were concerned, there was not another person on earth. Their world started and ended with each other. Just before dark, they both walked down to the lake and took a swim. The water was a little cold, but after being in the saddle all day, it felt great.

After the swim, they enjoyed the warmth of the campfire. Kay sat there, shivering. Joe reached over, picked up his coat and placed it over her shoulders. She just looked at him and smiled. That smile said, "Thank you."

Between them, words were not always necessary. They could see it in each other's eyes. Love starts at the top. When it reaches clear through you, it's completed. That was where they were. They could just look at each other. Words were redundant, just a look said it all.

As they relaxed, with a good fire burning and a cup of hot tea, Kay reached over and put her hand on Joe's leg. He turned and looked at his wife. Her smile was pure, as was his. He reached over and kissed her. As he sat there with his arm around her, that peaceful feeling entered him as it always did when he was close to her. He whispered in her ear, "I'm the luckiest guy in the world. Simply because I have you in my life."

Soon, they both got up. Joe went to check the horses while Kay gave the camp a once over. Grabbing their pistols, the two headed for the tent and their sleeping bags. As Joe slid into the sleeping bag, to his surprise, he could feel Kay's leg. She looked at him and smiled. Taking his wife in his arms, he gave her a long, very passionate kiss.

About 3:00 a.m., all hell broke loose.

A pack of wolves had run through their camp.

That was all it took.

The horses spooked and broke free. That startled the two of them awake. Joe grabbed his pistol and scrambled out of the sleeping bag and tent. Running toward the horses, he knew he was already too late. They had broken the picket line and were gone. Walking back to the tent, he threw a couple more pieces of wood on the fire.

Kay came out of the tent and looked at Joe. She started laughing. He was standing next to the fire with a pistol in his hand and a smile. When he heard the horses whinny and the yip of the wolves, he did not stop to get dressed. He just bolted for the horses.

Kay looked at him, still laughing, and said, "Joe, you might want to get dressed. Not that I mind you looking like that. Although it might be warmer if you had some clothes on. Plus, what if we meet someone?" She giggled.

Joe, looking down, smiled sheepishly, and walked into the tent. He came out a few minutes later, and Kay handed him a cup of coffee.

It was going to be a long day. They had to find the horses. There was no way they could get everything out. Not without at least one horse.

They sat drinking coffee as the eastern sky started changing colors. Sunrise in the late fall can be breathtakingly beautiful as the sky goes through several shades of red, starting with pink, a rose color, and finally red. As the sky was changing colors, Joe was getting ready to go.

He handed Kay her gun belt containing her pistol and extra ammunition. "In this country," he explained, "Being on foot, you can become part of the food chain."

Joe told Kay to grab both rifles, making sure to grab a box of ammunition for each while he grabbed a couple of lengths of rope and bucket with some grain in it.

Joe looked at the tracks, and off they went. "Those wolves must have really spooked the horses well," said Joe as he followed the tracks.

A couple of hours later, and still no sign of the horses. Nothing but tracks. They topped a small hill and took a break. Finding a couple of nice, comfy rocks to sit against, they looked at the surrounding countryside. With the fall showing off all the beautiful colors, it was fantastic.

Kay looked at Joe and said, "Will we find the horses?"

Joe looked at her and then away and said, "Yes, I'm sure we will."

Although in his mind, he doubted it. He did not want to scare her any more than she already was. They sat there for a few more minutes and started looking again. They made a huge circle and were back at the camp late that afternoon, tired from a long walk, with no luck.

Joe built a fire while Kay started getting something ready to eat. After dinner, they walked down to the lake again and took a swim.

Looking at Kay standing naked from the waist up caused a reaction in him. So, without saying a word, he slowly made his way to where she was. Joe picked her up and slowly let her slide down. She was having the same problem watching him. Carefully, they made their way to shore. They laid together in the grass. Taking her in his arms and kissing Kay, she responded instantly as her tongue found his.

Soon, his hands started to wander, her breathing increased, and her body reacted as it did every time. From the very first time. Joe knew what she wanted and needed from him.

He slowly kissed his way down, stopping at each breast, her flat, firm stomach, where he made circles with his tongue around her belly button, then continuing down. Kissing the inside of her thighs and flicking his tongue in just the right area. The wave started building and crashed as she cried out. Joe slowly started kissing his way back up, stopping, he took each engorged nipple into his mouth, letting his tongue work a circle around it as he sucked lightly at first, then harder until she placed her hand on the back of his head to hold him there. As her hand slid away, the wave broke again. She arched her back to receive him as he pushed in. It was instantaneous; the wave crested and broke. Again, she cried out. As Joe's rhythm increased, she met every thrust as wave after wave started building higher and higher and then crashing in a body-shuddering explosion. Joe's release came concurrently as he thrust harder and harder. As he slowed and stopped together, they laid together, totally spent in a state of erotic bliss. With her arms and legs wrapped around him, she was totally engulfed in what was happening. She loved the weight of Joe's body on top of her. Holding him in place, she relished the feeling.

Slowly, he rolled to the side, pulling her on top of him as he did. With his arms still around her, he kissed her deeply and romantically. Holding her there, he continued to kiss his way down her neck to her throat and back up. With another deep, romantic, loving kiss, he held onto her, hugging her tightly.

Twenty minutes later, they decided maybe they should clean up and possibly wash some clothes, then hang them to dry in camp.

Walking back toward their camp, Joe looked at Kay. With the look on her face and in her eyes, he could tell she was scared. Giving her a hug, he said, "Don't worry, I'll protect you, and we will get out of here."

Together, they washed their clothes, then hung them to dry and sat around the fire, drinking tea. They were both tired after the long walk and exercise down by the lake. Sitting by the fire, they enjoyed a cup of tea and relaxed.

Bedtime came earlier than normal. Putting more wood on the fire, Joe banked it to ensure it would last all night, and they crawled into bed. Joe put his arms around Kay, pulling her close, and they were both soon fast asleep.

Joe's sleep was broken with disturbing dreams of jungles, mountains, and men with guns trying to kill him.

He was running again, down a narrow mountain trail. The Taliban had found him. With his camp only a mile away, he was running in the other direction. He didn't want them to find his camp. He ran as hard as he could while trying to call for help. There was a patrol of Rangers in the area, and he was trying to get to them and the help they would provide. With his rifle slung across his back, he ran uphill like a goat, using his arms and hands, as well as his legs.

Nearing the top, he slowed, and just as he topped the hill, the Taliban opened up. Randy dove over the top and rolled down the other side. Finding a small cave, he backed in and set up for a fight. Pushing a couple of large rocks into the opening, nothing short of a direct hit from a rocket-propelled grenade would get him out of there. As the Taliban started working their way up the mountainside towards him, Randy waited.

Sticking only the barrel out, he waited.

When the patrol was about fifty yards below him, he

opened up, killing four in the first few seconds. Pulling back, he waited for them to empty their guns and popped out again. With careful shot placement, he killed a couple more. Then he heard the whoosh of a rocket-propelled grenade. He managed to duck back into the cave just as it exploded above him. Still back in the small cave, he heard another hit below him.

They were getting closer.

With dust and debris still in the air, he popped out again and opened up. He hit one more, then ducking back, he grabbed two grenades. Pulling the pins, he popped up and tossed both. The patrol saw him and started shooting just as they both went off. Everything went quiet, and he slowly moved forward, looking over the edge. He could see several dead bodies lying in the area. Carefully, he sighted downhill and waited.

In a few minutes, they slowly started moving. Randy carefully sighted and squeezed the trigger several more times. Everything on the mountain side ceased to move.

Joe's eyes opened, and he carefully looked around.

Something was moving outside the tent.

Looking to his side, he saw Kay. Letting out his breath, he slowly calmed down. Joe quietly slid out of the sleeping bag, grabbing his pistol. He opened the tent flap and stepped out. One of the three horses had wandered back. Grabbing the lead rope, he walked slowly up to it and snapped the rope to her halter. Walking back to camp with the horse in tow, he tied her to a nearby tree, then went looking for the picket line.

Kay stepped out of the tent, as he approached, looking at her, he said, "That was easy enough. One down, two to go."

After they had something to eat and a couple of cups of coffee, they got ready and left again, looking for the remaining horses.

They spent all day looking again. They saw everything but horses. It was beautiful and heartbreaking. Arriving back at camp, they found that an unwanted intruder had been there. From the tracks and smell, Joe knew it was a wolverine. It had made a total mess of everything.

Wolverines are ferocious members of the weasel family. They have been known to drive larger predators off their kills, such as wolves and even bears. They fear nothing and can eat almost anything, from fresh kills to something that has been dead a couple of weeks or more, as well as grasses and berries. Nature's garbage disposal.

Joe and Kay spent the next couple of hours looking through their gear. The wolverine had made a mess, chewing through leather, just tearing everything apart. It tore a hole in the tent, it pulled their clean clothes off the line, and it tore open their food supply. The only thing it did not destroy was the sleeping bag, yet it crapped on it. Joe pulled it out of the tent and walked to the lake. This stinking thing needed a bath. After throwing it in the lake, he put a couple of rocks on it so it would not float away, and he went back to the camp and helped Kay salvage what they could.

Then they went back to the lake to try to clean the sleeping bags. With the two of them, they managed to do a fairly good job. Although Joe knew he would throw them away when they got out of there.

Joe rigged up a couple of ropes to put them over, then built two small fires to help dry them. It was going to be a damp, cold night for them if it did not get good and dry.

It was a good thing they got back to camp early after going through everything. After they had saved everything they could, it was far after dark before they finally headed to bed. Pulling Kay close, they lay there talking about where they would go in the morning.

Joe thought about what lay ahead. He knew they were in trouble. It would be a long walk out if they did not find the horses.

The night was full of dreams, and Joe woke several times. Waiting and listening as the sounds of the night came to him. With his mind having been trained to listen for danger, laying perfectly still was a must.

The morning brought the same thing: Up early, eat, and head out looking for the other two horses. They went in a different direction that day. Seeing a large rock outcropping, they sat in the shade and rested.

Looking up, Joe said, "I think I'll climb this and get a better look around."

From the top, he could see for miles.

Pointing, he called to Kay, saying, "Hey, look over there. I think I can see them." Joe knew better, but in his haste to get down, he slipped, lost his balance, and fell the last twenty feet bouncing off the rock, there was a loud snap. He knew he had broken his arm. Kay spun around, and in a few steps, she was at his side, just as he was trying to sit up. He looked at Kay, who was now kneeling, trying to hold him in place. She had tears in her eyes. She knew they were in trouble.

She helped Joe to his feet and together, they slowly headed back to camp. Joe could feel where the bone had broken. It felt like a clean break. He was sure with her help, together, they could set the bone. Pausing and taking both of her hands in his one good one, he said, "Kay, you're going to have to help me set this arm."

Her eyes snapped open, and she said, "No! No! No way! I can't. I can't do that. I have no idea what I'm doing."

Joe said, "Now listen to me. You have to. It has to be set. I'll explain what I want you to do. We will talk about it, and I'll show you where to grab it and what to do. If we can set it, I'll be able to help somewhat. If we don't and it starts to heal, I'll be in severe pain and absolutely worthless. Also, it will mean surgery when we get back to Kalispell."

After they got to camp, Kay first made sure Joe was comfortable. Next, she started the fire and put the coffee on.

Then, turning back to Joe, she said, "Okay, what's next? What do you need me to do?"

Joe said, "Get two pieces of wood about as long as my lower arm. Then grab one of my shirts. We need to cut it into two-inch wide strips."

Kay got up, getting Joe a cup of coffee. Next, she went through the woodpile until she found two slabs that should work. Laying them next to Joe, she watched.

Joe said, "Reach over there and get me that hatchet. We'll split this one and they'll be perfect." Placing the hatchet, he said, "Take the axe and hit the hatchet." They split one off a larger piece, making two long, flat narrow slabs. Turning, she next went into the tent and, going through his clothes, she found one of his shirts she didn't like. Walking back, she poured a second cup for herself. She sat down next to Joe and kissed him on the cheek. Looking around for a second, she said, "Okay, we have three slabs for the brace. Oh, and here, let's use this shirt."

"Oh, Kay, that's my favorite shirt. Why that one?" Chuckling, he continued, "I'm only kidding, honey. That will work fine. Here's my knife, cut through the stitching. Then tear it into strips, say two-inches wide and a couple of feet long. Oh and please be careful. That knife is razor sharp."

Kay cut the shirt, then tore it into several strips. With everything ready, Joe lifted his arm and, pointing at the inside of his elbow, he said, "You will need to put your foot here.

Then grab my wrist like this." He carefully placed his hand on his wrist. Continuing, he said, "Use both hands. When I say pull, don't stop pulling no matter what until I say stop."

Kay looked at Joe's arm and said, "Please, Joe, there has to be another way. I can't do this. I don't want to hurt you."

Joe looked directly into Kay's eyes and said, "I know you would never hurt me on purpose, although now you have to. You have to do this. A little pain now will keep me from being in a lot of pain later. Now please, when we start, don't look at me, look at what you are doing. You need to put your foot against my arm just above my elbow, then grab my wrist and pull with both hands. I'm going to try to squeeze the bone back into place. If this works, the bone will settle back into alignment and heal properly." Then he kissed Kay and said, "Honey, please don't look at me."

Joe took a piece of leather and bit down on it, hoping to stop himself from screaming. He knew if he screamed, she would stop. This was going to hurt beyond belief.

They moved things around, and Joe laid down on top of the sleeping bags. He looked at Kay and said, "Now, one more thing, if I pass out, feel my arm. Make sure it feels like the other one, then put the sticks on both sides and wrap the strips of cloth around a couple of times. Make sure they are tight. Then tie the ends together. They need to be tight enough to hold the bone in place but not stop the blood flow. Then just leave me asleep until I wake up."

Kay took hold of his wrist, putting her foot against his upper arm. Pausing for a minute, she said, "Please Lord, I love this man. Give me the strength I need to do this."

Then, with a look from Joe, she pulled. Joe bit down as hard as he could on the leather. Then, squeezing his arm, he felt the bone slide into place. The pain was beyond what he thought he could endure. Dropping his face into the sleeping bag, he blacked out.

Kay did what Joe said, feeling both arms, making sure they felt the same. She took the sticks, placing one on the top and bottom, then taking the strips of cloth from Joe's shirt, she wrapped the strips around his arm and tied the ends. Then she just sat by her husband, rubbed his neck, stroked his hair, and cried.

Joe came to about half an hour later. She got up and made him supper and tea, putting a liberal amount of painkiller in his tea. Then she picked everything up, did a double take, making sure everything was okay, banked the fire like Joe had shown her, put more wood on it, and crawled in next to him. Joe was still in severe pain and had the start of a very restless night.

After Kay knew he was sleeping, she got up on her elbow, stroked his hair and cried.

She knew they were in trouble, but she also knew that Joe would do everything in his power to protect her and get them out of the mess they were in. Finally, being cried out, she laid down as close as she could get and drifted off.

Kay woke up before Joe. Carefully, she slid out of the sleeping bag and out of the tent. Standing still for a minute, she gazed at the surrounding mountains and the beauty of the Montana wilderness. Then, putting more wood on the fire, she walked to the lake and filled the coffeepot to make coffee. Grabbing the small camp shovel, she scooped hot coals from the fire and placed the cast iron frying pan directly on them. Opening the food cooler, she placed several strips of bacon in the pan. She sliced up a medium size potato and started making breakfast.

Joe's eyes started to flutter as he woke to the smell of coffee and bacon. He slowly crawled out of the tent, saying, "Something smells fantastic."

Slowly, he walked across the campsite. Kay glanced over at her husband and, getting up, she helped him to where they had been sitting so he could lean back against a log they had rolled into place. Getting him settled, she got him a cup of coffee, adding another liberal amount of the painkiller. Bringing him his coffee, she then made up two plates, walked back and sat next to him. They enjoyed breakfast in silence.

Joe looked around for a minute and smiled as he looked back at Kay and said, "Thank God it was my right and not my left!" Laughing, he added, "I can still feed myself plus do a few other things. I'm not sure where the horses went. Maybe we should go through our supplies and keep only what we absolutely have to have and head back for Kalispell."

Kay looked from her plate and met Joe's eyes. Smiling, she replied, "That sounds like a great idea. You need a doctor and Joe, I have to admit, I am just a little scared."

Joe smiled and said, "It doesn't hurt much, and I'm sure you did a great job. We'll be just fine. The weather shouldn't get really bad for a month or more, plus we have plenty of food and other supplies."

After getting dressed, Joe started going through the remaining supplies. Making two piles, he told Kay, "Burn everything we are not taking."

After that, they started repacking so, between the horse and two backpacks, they could carry everything. Joe packed so that everything they needed daily was in one pack. He also put all the food in one pack that the horse would carry. He then placed both of their rifles on the packs, so they would still be readily available. Once they finished repacking and getting everything ready except the tent and sleeping bags, Joe looked at the sky and said, "We can leave early in the morning. It's already afternoon, and we would not get very far."

With the fire still burning, Joe threw a couple more pieces of wood on it and Kay filled the coffeepot again. Adding coffee, she placed it on the fire and sat next to Joe. She asked, "What do you think happened to the other two horses?"

Joe looked around and said, "I'm guessing they probably

went home."

"Really?" Kay asked. "Would they know their way home?"

Joe replied, "Yeah. I'm sure they can find their way from here."

Kay made a light supper. They continued to talk about the hike out as they ate.

After they finished eating, Kay said, "You just sit here and rest. I'll get this cleaned up and make us some tea."

Joe tried to help with the cleanup, although Kay had a complete fit, saying, "If you don't get out of the way, I'll break your other arm. Now go sit down and get the hell out of the way."

After she was done with the cleanup, she made tea. Again, she added painkiller to Joe's. They sat enjoying the fire, the tea, and the love they shared. With everything ready and the fact they had work most of the day, Kay said, "It's getting late. I think we had better be heading for the tent and sleep."

Joe was exhausted after the day they had. Kay, however, lay awake until Joe's breathing leveled out and she knew he was sleeping. Then slowly and carefully, she sat up cross-legged and watched her sleeping husband while stroking his hair or just laying her hand on his chest. Finally, she laid down next to him. She just couldn't get close enough. She was scared. She knew Joe would give his life to protect her. She also knew she would do the same for him. She loved him that much. Completely all the way through.

***

In the morning, Kay made a fast breakfast and coffee. It was going to be a long walk out. She knew Joe would do too much and hurt his arm again, so as they loaded up, she kept an eye on him, not letting him pick up the heavy things alone. Joe noticed Kay trying to help him.

He smiled and thought, *She sure is a fantastic lady.*

Together, they worked on getting ready to head out; he looked over at Kay and smiled. She smiled back. That was all there was. Two smiles said it all.

It was still early morning when they started their walk out. It would take them four or five days if everything went well. Joe swung his arms as he walked. Soon, he started holding it still and bent at the elbow.

Kay noticed that almost immediately. So, looking around, she found his cut-up shirt. Stopping for a couple of minutes, she made a sling. Placing it around his neck, and gently picked up his right arm and slid it into the sling. Then, looking at him, she smiled and said, "Now keep it there."

Joe looked at the sling Kay had made for him. Smiling, he thought, *I had better listen to her, or I bet she will break my other arm.*

They made good time the first day and stopped an hour or so before dark. Joe started trying to set up the tent while Kay took care of the horse. She tied it to the picket line and hurried to help. They soon finished with the tent and had a fire going. Shortly after, they ate supper and enjoyed a cup of tea. Kay spiked Joe's with a little extra painkiller, hoping it would help him sleep better, or at least get some.

She noticed the night before he had been very restless. She was sure he was having disturbing dreams. After supper, they cleaned up the camp, putting everything away, and crawled into the sleeping bag. Kay again laid awake until she knew Joe was sleeping. Again, she propped herself up on an elbow and just watched her sleeping husband.

Joe's night was full of dreams. Although he did something totally new. He started talking and Kay laid awake, listening. At first, it didn't make any sense but as the night continued, she started remembering he had talked to her while in Alaska. Something about a part of him she didn't know. Something very few people knew he had said.

Kay laid there thinking about and trying to remember what he talked about while she lay in his lap. Drifting in and out. She remembered him talking about Afghanistan and Colombia.

Could that be what's causing his nightmares? she wondered.

Still laying there, she slowly sat up. *He said the military honed his shooting skills. The only people I know of that can shoot like that are snipers. Is he trained as a sniper? If so, is that what is causing some of these terrible nightmares?*

In the morning, they had a quick breakfast and coffee and

got an early start. They were both watching the sky. Something did not look right, and shortly before noon, they knew what it was. A fall snowstorm was blowing in and, in a matter of a few minutes, there was a foot of snow with no sign of letting up. The wind was picking up, making visibility almost zero.

Joe said, "We need to find a place to camp, and now."

They found a place underneath a rock outcropping. Joe told Kay to dig a snow cave.

Shortly after she started the first one, it caved in, burying her alive. Joe ran over and dug her out. Reaching in, he grabbed her and pulled her out and, helping her up, he said, "Dig it deep. Follow the ground as much as you can."

He got the packs off the horse and tied it to a nearby tree. Then putting all their supplies next to another tree where they could easily be found. Dragging the tent, he helped Kay get it inside the snow cave. Then he went back after the sleeping bags and guns. He also grabbed their water, a long stick, and finally, the cooler.

Kay looked at him funny, then asked, "What is all this?"

Joe pushed the sleeping bags inside and said, "Get in there. I'll explain after we are inside."

Then he pushed the water in and backed in himself, pulling the stick in as he went. Kay noticed it was too long, but before she could say anything, Joe said, "Perfect."

Then he reached out and pulled the cooler right into the

opening. He turned on a small flashlight as he helped Kay get the bags zipped together. The night was going to be a little cold, but he knew they would survive.

After everything was done, he said, "Get out of your wet clothes and into the bag." Using the light, he watched as she got undressed.

Wow! he thought. Every time he watched her get undressed, it would cause a reaction in him. He could not believe how lucky he was and how great she looked.

After Kay was inside, he undressed, laying both of their wet clothes on top of the bag. He reached inside his pack and got out a small can. Kay looked at him with a puzzled look and asked, "What is that?"

Joe looked at her and explained, "This is Sterno, this small can will keep it warm enough to keep us from freezing. It burns clear or blue. Giving off nearly zero carbon monoxide. It will keep us warm until we go to sleep." Pausing as he lit it, he continued, "The cooler blocks the wind, but it also marks the way out."

She asked, "Okay, now what about the stick?"

Joe said, "It will keep a breathing hole open, allowing fresh air in so we don't suffocate. Just push the stick forward and back to open an air passage. If you wake up during the night just move the stick. If you wake with a headache, wake me immediately."

Kay asked, "Why? What would a headache mean?"

Joe replied, "Oxygen deprivation. A lack of oxygen gets to your brain. If you get a headache, we need a larger breathing hole. Although I'm sure with the way it's set up, what we already have will be more than enough."

Kay looked at Joe with a look of pure astonishment. She would never have thought of all that, and Joe never looked better. She knew, broken arm and all, he would get her safely out of the mountains.

She looked at the Sterno and asked, "Won't that melt the snow?"

Joe said, "Some, but it will cause a layer of ice to form on the roof of our little snow fort. What does melt will run under the tent with us being on top, we should stay high and dry."

Again, she smiled and thought, *He sure knows the outdoors.* Then she asked, "Have you ever done this before?"

He laughed and said, "Yes, many times." Then he told her about building one in the Arctic once. A really bad storm caught him and another guy out on the ice. They cut snow blocks and made a type of Eskimo igloo. It took about half an hour. It wasn't really good, but they stayed warm and out of the weather.

She looked at him and said, "You never told me about that. When did that happen?"

Joe smiled as he replied, "While chasing that polar bear last spring."

She smiled and thought, *I wonder how many other close*

calls he's had that he's never told me about?

Either Kay or Joe would move the stick every hour or so, keeping the fresh air coming inside. As morning broke, so did the storm. Joe was dressed and poked a small hole in the snow to see outside.

"Clear and blue," he said.

As Kay was getting dressed, he pushed the cooler out of the way, opening their overnight hiding place.

Most of the snow that had fallen during the night had been blown into larger drifts. The horse was grazing about fifty feet away. He looked up as Joe climbed out of the snow cave.

Joe found their gear and started looking for wood to make fire. He was able to find firewood, although the smaller wood needed to start a fire was all wet. Joe walked over to a bunch of pine trees. The lower branches were dry, and even some of the lower green branches would burn. After breaking off enough branches, he walked back to where they wanted to make the fire, and in a matter of just a few minutes, he had a fire burning.

Giving the fire time to get going, Kay filled the coffeepot with water. Adding the coffee, she put it on the fire to boil. Then she started making some breakfast as Joe pulled everything out of their snow cave. After rolling up the sleeping bags and tent, he attached them to the backpacks. Walking over, he got the horses loaded and had everything ready, as Kay called him to eat.

Joe walked over, looked at Kay, and smiled. *How could she look that great after sleeping in a snow cave in the middle of a storm?* He knew she was an amazing woman. He also knew he would give his life to protect her.

As they ate, Joe looked around.

And then Kay screamed.

He jumped up and spun around.

A black bear had smelled their food and gotten a little too close. Joe grabbed his pistol while looking for his rifle. He told Kay to stay still. He slowly walked to where the rifle was and jacked a shell into the chamber.

He then walked back and stood in front of Kay. The bear looked at them and slowly turned and walked away. Joe looked back at where the horse should be. It was standing stone still, eyes wide open, ears forward, watching the bear. "Wow!" Joe said, "Thank God it didn't break the rope and run off again!"

Slowly, he walked toward the horse. Petting her slowly calmed the animal down. Then, untying the horse, he led him closer to the camp. With everything cleaned up, he finished loading the horse. Kay helped him get his pack on, and he helped her. With everything loaded off, they went. They still had a long walk ahead of them.

They talked as they walked, stopping whenever they got tired or just needed a break. Looking at the surrounding scenery made the day go by while still making it close to ten miles.

Looking at Kay, he said, "If we keep up this pace, we should be out of here in a couple more days."

Late that afternoon, they topped a hill and stopped. Holding perfectly still, they watched as a large herd of elk was grazing on the downhill side. As they stood there watching, a large bull walked out of the timber and bugled. Joe pointed to where the bull was standing.

Looking at Kay, he said, "Sure wish I had an elk license. That is enough meat to last us a year."

She smiled and said, "Yes, and great eating also."

As the herd passed by, Joe saw something that made him smile. Two horses stood there, looking their way.

Slowly, he touched Kay's arm and pointed, saying," Look over there. Are those horses?"

Looking, Kay said, "Yes! But are they *our* horses?"

Joe said, "There's only one way to find out."

Taking the packhorse, they started that way. The horses stood there looking at them for a few minutes, then trotted out of sight.

Joe swore under his breath and said, "Probably mustangs. There are some around here."

They changed direction and headed back toward the trail out.

As they walked, Joe asked, "Is it getting warmer?"

Kay stopped and looked at Joe. He was starting to sweat.

She said, "Yes, I think so."

They kept walking.

When Joe said, "I think we are getting close to where we have to cross that small creek."

A few minutes later, they walked around the corner; Joe swore and said, "I think we are in trouble."

The small creek was about twenty-five feet wide and running hard. Looking at the current, he just shook his head.

Joe found a stout pole and removed his pants and boots. Taking a long rope, he tied one end around his waist and the other end to the horse.

Looking at Kay, he said, "If I lose my balance, use the horse to pull me back to shore."

Kay looked shocked, although she trusted him and his judgment. He slowly walked into the water, and by the time he was in the middle, he turned around and headed back.

He looked at Kay, saying, "It's going to be cold. Although if we are careful, I think we can get across it." Then he turned to the horse, saying, "What about you? Are you going to give us any trouble?"

He turned as she started removing her pants.

Joe said, "Leave your boots on. Those rocks may be sharp, and we can camp on the other side and dry everything tonight."

Kay sat down and put her boots back on, and Joe took a shorter rope, tying her to him. Then they headed into the water. As they crossed, the water got deeper on the other side. It was above Joe's waist and nearly to Kay's chest. Kay was upstream from Joe. This way, if she slipped or was carried away by the current, he could hopefully catch her before the rope went tight. He wasn't sure if he could keep his footing with her caught in the current.

Just as they got to the other side, Joe slipped and went down. He tried to grab the rocks, but his rope pulled Kay off her feet and underwater. Joe quickly found footing and got up. He knew Kay could not swim. He also knew by now she would be really scared. Using both arms, he grabbed her as she passed, pulling her to her feet and pushing her toward shore. Joe was still downstream, and the horse was on the shore. As Kay stumbled again, he grabbed her, pulling her up, and she made it to shore.

Looking upstream, he saw a log headed down the creek. Knowing he was about to be hit by it, he pulled his knife and cut the rope between him and Kay. With the rope cut, he turned to try to get out of the way.

The log swept him downstream.

Kay saw what had happened and turned the horse just before the rope got tight. Joe was dragged underwater as the log passed over him. He felt a sharp, stabbing pain in his upper thigh. Coming up, he regained his footing and made it to shore about thirty feet downstream.

Kay ran towards him, looking to see if he had been hurt.

Joe looked at her, and he could tell from the look on her face that something was wrong. Looking down, he saw blood running out of a huge gash in his upper leg. Joe quickly put his hand on it, trying to slow the flow.

Turning, he quickly walked back into the water and stood there while the cold water cleaned and numbed his leg.

He told Kay, "Get the first aid kit and look if there's a needle. We need to put a few stitches in this."

As she ran back to the horse, he continued to stand in the ice cold water. He knew the cold water would numb his leg enough so she could sew the cut closed at the same time, flushing and hopefully cleaning the wound. He was still in the water when Kay got back.

He said, "Get everything ready so you can stitch this while it is still numb from the water."

When everything was ready, she called, "Okay, come on, let's get you patched up again."

Joe walked out of the water, holding his hand over the gash. The ice-cold water had slowed the blood flow by making everything shrink.

Before each stitch, she squeezed a little triple antibiotic cream onto the wound. Joe never felt a thing. The cold water had worked. Although he knew it would hurt later.

Next, they needed a fire, and quick. Joe and Kay walked around, collecting twigs, moss, pine needles, anything that would catch quickly. Joe managed to find some dry wood, and he hauled an armload back with him.

Kay asked, "Hey, where did you find that? Is there any more?"

Joe pointed and said, "Yeah, there's a big pile of drift wood about fifty feet upstream, just after that bend in the creek."

She jogged off up the riverbank, making several trips. In a few minutes, Joe had a big fire started. After they had a good supply of wood and a hot fire, everything started calming down.

Joe got up and started unpacking the horse and got the pack with all their daily needs. He set up the tent while Kay started getting supper ready. Then he put the sleeping bags in place and then hobbled back and forth, hauling more wood.

After supper, with everything cleaned up, Kay made tea. She spiked Joe's with a good amount of the only painkiller they had left. Then Kay made Joe sit down while she straightened out the sleeping bags so, hopefully, they could get some much-needed sleep. Joe hobbled around, getting both pistols and putting them in the tent in their usual spots. He then grabbed both rifles and put them against a log next to the tent. Kay could tell the painkiller wasn't doing a very good job. Although Joe would never sit anything out. He did everything he normally did, just a bit slower.

Joe sat sipping his tea and staring into the fire. Every now and then, he would look around. He knew they were in trouble. Kay could not get the two of them out of there.

Finally, he looked at her and said, "I think it's getting close to bedtime. I'm sure I'll be a little sore tomorrow, but we will make a few miles anyway."

Kay took her normal position and lay awake until she knew Joe was sleeping. Then, with tears in her eyes, she gently stroked his hair. Joe was an incredibly strong guy with a high tolerance to pain. She knew he would do what it took to get them out of this mess. After a while, she laid down and crawled closer to Joe. She just knew she needed to be closer. With one hand on his chest, she drifted off to sleep.

Joe had a very restless night. His leg hurt him something terrible. He dreamed about being in Afghanistan.

He had been shot in the left leg. The bullet had gone clear through, but he had to stop the bleeding. Tearing a length of his shirt off, he pushed it into the bullet hole from both sides. Then he took another length and wrapped it around, holding what was left of his shirt in place. Then he got up and under the cover of darkness, using his night vision goggles, he carefully walked the five plus miles to his high mountain camp, setting up several defensive traps along the way.

He started a fire and placed a half inch metal stake in the fire. Carefully, he removed the makeshift bandage he had put on. The worst part was pulling the cloth out of the wound. Picking up the metal stake, he looked at it. It was glowing red for nearly half its eighteen-inch length. Taking a deep breath, he pushed the stake into the bullet wound from the inside of his leg, going towards the outside. Pulling it out, he placed it back in the fire. Breathing hard and shaking nearly out of control, he knew he was only half done. Laying there, he kept a bandage on the outside to help stop the bleeding. Picking up the stake, he took a deep breath and pushed it into his leg again. This time when he pulled it out, he dropped it to the ground, laid back, and fell asleep. He woke to an explosion. Someone or something had tripped one of the bombs.

Crawling across his hidden camp, he grabbed his M16 and several extra clips. Then he made his way to where he could see down the trail. To get ready for what he thought for sure was going to be a fight. With the sky lightening in the east, Randy saw movement.

He watched as they started trying to work their way up the trail that led to the top. With several traps set on the trail, he was sure they would never make it. The traps he set would kill most, if not all, of them. As they tripped the second bomb, they soon started spreading out across the face of the mountain, working their way from rock to rock. Randy could now see them without the aid of his night vision.

Making sure the suppressor was tight, he placed the red dot on the closest and touched the trigger. A red mist appeared, spraying the nearby rocks with blood and brain matter as the .62-grain entered high on the left side of his head, exiting just below his ear, taking most of the right side with it.

With deadly accurate shot placement and the booby traps, the fight was over in twenty minutes. Randy crawled back, picking up his radio. He called for help.

Morning broke, and Kay felt for Joe. He was gone. She bolted upright, then scrambled out of the tent. He was sitting by the fire, drinking coffee. She stood and walked across the camp topless. Joe looked at her and smiled, saying, "Honey, that's a great idea, but I don't think my leg would agree."

She said, "I was checking on you. I woke up and you were gone." Then she looked down and said, "Oops." Turning around, she went back into the tent and got dressed.

Joe thought, *Wow, she looks absolutely fantastic!*

Kay started breakfast while Joe was making a crutch to help him walk. They packed everything, loaded up, and started out. Kay watched as Joe walked. She could tell his leg was hurting.

Earlier than normal, she said, "Joe, I'm tired. Can we stop and rest?" Then she said, "There's a creek right there. Let's stay here tonight. There is plenty of wood and water."

Joe looked at Kay and said, "Great idea. My leg hurts some, anyway. No sense in overdoing it."

They worked together to find firewood. While Joe started a fire, Kay walked down and filled their water supply. After getting water on to boil, she made supper.

Joe hobbled around, finding more firewood, and finally, he sat down to relax by the fire. Kay made tea and loaded his with as much painkiller as she thought was safe. After a hot meal and all the painkillers she had put in his tea, Joe was starting to relax a little.

Kay got up and put both pistols in the tent and the rifles in their place by the fire. Picking up his empty cup, she filled it again, and this time, she put about half what she had put in the first. Then, filling hers, she snuggled up next to him and together, they sat and watched the fire. Joe started to fall asleep when Kay said, "Joe, I think we had better get in the tent. If you fall asleep out here, I could never get you in there. Let alone covered up."

Slowly, Joe made his way to the tent. Kay then helped him get undressed and into the sleeping bag. She did a once over of the camp and double checked, making sure everything was put away. Then she crawled in with Joe. He was already sleeping. She smiled. The painkiller was working. She just sat cross-legged and watched him sleep. After an hour or so, she crawled in next to him and, with her arm across his chest, she drifted off.

Joe's night was terrible.

He tossed and turned, then screamed, "You assholes are shelling me. Cease fire, for Christ's sake, stop. Cease fire," he screamed again and again.

Kay bolted upright and sat, scared to move. She listened as Joe continued to talk, scream, swear, and pray. With tears in her eyes, she sat. Slowly, she slid her hand onto his chest.

This seemed to calm him down, then suddenly he screamed, "I'm hit, I'm hit." Thrashing around, he grabbed something and started moving like he was shooting at something. Kay continued to rub his chest and stroke his hair.

Finally, he calmed down.

Slowly, she laid down next to him. She could feel he was warm.

Joe was really stiff in the morning, but he managed to help get things packed. After a fast breakfast and coffee, off they went.

Kay asked, "When do you think we will be out of here? I want you to go to the doctor as soon as you can."

Joe smiled and said, "Hopefully late Friday or sometime Saturday."

It was Monday.

Kay wanted to just sit down and cry. She hated seeing him in this much pain.

Again, early afternoon, she asked, "Can we stop?"

She knew Joe would keep going and push himself way too hard. She did not care if it was Saturday or next Tuesday, as long as they got out alive and that he would be alright. That's all that mattered.

They found a place to camp about an hour down the trail. Again, Joe started looking for firewood. Kay unpacked the horse and tied him to a picket line. Then she helped Joe. They got a fire started and walked down to the creek to wash up.

They tried to clean up every night when water was available. It really felt great. Joe lowered his pants, and Kay said, "Hey, Joe, not here. There might be people around."

Joe started laughing and said, "Now, wouldn't that be funny? We haven't seen a person in two weeks! Although you are correct, if we did, we would."

Kay just laughed until she saw the cut. It looked like it was getting infected.

Kay made supper again and spiked Joe's tea with a painkiller. Then he helped her get everything ready so they could get some sleep. Joe put the rifles in place. Kay grabbed the pistols and Joe crawled into the sleeping bag.

Kay again gave the camp a once over, making sure everything was put away. She walked over and checked the horse. Going back to the tent, she crawled in. Joe was already sleeping. She slowly slid in next to him, snuggled up close, and stroked his hair while watching him sleep.

He was in immense pain. She felt his chest and forehead. He was getting warmer and warmer. Getting up, she found the water and, soaking an old shirt, she folded it and placed it on his forehead. Taking another old shirt, she soaked it and started wiping his arms and face.

Kay woke up early. She carefully sat up and pushed off the sleeping bag. Then, looking at the gash in his leg, it was all swollen up and red. She touched it, and Joe jumped as the pain shot through him like a knife. She laid back down, took a deep breath, then got up.

Joe started waking up. His bladder was full. He needed to get outside, like now.

Crawling out of the tent, he started to stand and lost his balance. Kay was just a couple of feet away, and as Joe started to fall, she was there, trying to keep him from hitting the ground hard.

He started to crawl, dragging his sore leg.

Kay said, "Joe, let me help you."

She helped him to his feet and as he turned around, Kay gasped. "Oh my God, honey! What are we going to do?"

Joe shook his head, trying to clear his thoughts, and asked, "What are you going to do about what?"

Kay stood there and pointed. Joe looked down and carefully walked back to camp. Sitting down, he says, "It needs to be opened."

Kay replied, "I can't do it."

He then added, "We need some hot water to clean the poison and infection off as it comes out." Handing her his hunting knife, he continued, "Put this in the fire. When the blade is red hot, you need to cut my leg open so it can drain."

Then, laying his head back, he drifted off.

Kay still looked at his leg. Finally, looking at him like he was nuts, she said, "Oh no, not me, I'm not! No, no, no!"

Joe mumbled, "You have to. I can't! This is going to really hurt."

Kay sat down and said, "I'm sure, but no. I know I can't."

Looking at Joe, she realized he had passed out.

Kay took the knife and laid it in the fire. She then walked over, filled the water pot, and put it on the fire to heat.

Next, with tears running down her face, she said, "I can't, honey. I can't! Please, Joe, there has to be something else." She looked at him again. He was out. *Oh, no,* she thought.

Getting everything ready, she took the cold water and, soaking an old shirt, she started wiping his face and neck again.

She stood there looking at him and said, "Oh, Lord, give me strength. I love you, Joe."

Kay took the knife. With the blade glowing red hot, she cut Joe's leg. The second the blade touched his skin, every muscle in Joe's body went rock hard. The infection exploded out of his leg. It went everywhere. Kay looked at Joe. He was just releasing his breath, although he had never said a word. Looking closer, she could tell he was still unconscious.

Kay poured the water on his leg, letting it wash the poison, infection, and blood away. Soon, it slowed and stopped.

Putting the knife back in the fire, she got more water. Then, looking at the cut in his leg, she said, "I'm going to have to do that again and keep doing it until there's no more infection." Looking at her husband lying there helpless was all she could stand. She knew what he would do. Taking a deep breath, she got ready.

Kay was crying as she crawled up and, holding the knife, she said, "Joe. Do you know how much this hurts me to hurt you?"

Sobbing, she slowly got up and took the knife out of the fire. The water had cooled down; she walked back over to Joe.

Kay took the knife and cut his leg again. As she cut, Joe would go rigid, then slowly relaxed. She would clean the wound each time after opening it. She kept this up a few more times until only blood came from the cut. Using a red-hot knife would cauterize the wound. This slowed some of the bleeding while allowing the infection to drain. Kay sat next to him all day, soaking the shirt, and trying to cool him down.

She knew he was still burning up. His fever was way too high. Finally, she took the knife and cut away his t-shirt. She sat and stared at his chest. There were many bullet wounds and knife scars. She put her hand on the scars and cried as she continued to hold cool, water-soaked shirts on him.

She walked to the stream many times, getting cooler water while always having hot water to bathe the gash in his leg.

Joe would mumble from time to time, along with screaming and swearing. A few times, he stiffened, arching his back and screaming.

Slowly, she pulled him up and stared at more scars on his back. Grabbing the wet shirt, she soaked it again and placed it on his back, then allowed him to sit back.

This went on all day and well into the night. Kay would

put wood on the fire. She kept water heating to clean the wound along with keeping cool water for compresses on his back and chest while wiping his face, forehead, and neck.

Finally, early in the morning, his fever broke.

Kay placed her hand on his forehead. It felt about the same as hers. With fresh cool water, she soaked the shirt on his back along with the one on his chest. Checking his forehead one more time, she laid down next to him and drifted off to sleep, only to wake an hour later to do it again.

She checked on him several times during the following day, catching short naps here and there.

Later that day, Kay collected more firewood. Then she made Joe something to eat. Trying to get him to eat was another story. Although she did get him to swallow a few bites. Fixing him some tea, again, she spiked it with a painkiller, allowing it to cool before trying to get him to drink some.

She cleaned up the camp. Joe was still sleeping, so Kay sat there, stroking his hair, and silently crying. Soon, she laid down by his side and continued to cry until she fell asleep.

Morning broke cool and clear. Kay was up, putting more wood on the fire, and had the coffee going. Joe slowly sat up, looking around. Slowly, he got up and limped over to her. Wrapping his arms around her, Kay said, "Oh my God, you're up. Why are you up? Get back over there and sit down."

Joe replied, "Yes, I'm up. Have I told you how much I love

you?"

Looking up at him, she smiled and said, "Not today. So, tell me that again. I'll never get sick of hearing it. Now, really! How are you feeling?"

Joe looked into Kay's eyes and said, "I promise we will get through this."

Smiling, Kay carefully walked Joe back to where he had been for the last two days. Turning, she started to cry as she made breakfast.

Joe looked at his leg and said, "What happened? The last thing I remember is telling you to cut my leg open."

Kay looked back at him and said, "That was two days ago."

Joe looked around and said, "Two days? What do you mean two days?"

Then, looking at his chest, he grabbed a wet t-shirt and tried to cover himself, saying, "Would you please get me another shirt?"

Kay stood, walking over to him. She sat down and said, "You had a terrible high fever. I've been keeping cool compresses on you while trying to keep that gash clean and draining. I had to cut your shirt off. I've seen your scars and bullet wounds. We can talk about that later. Although you are going to tell me!"

Joe looked at Kay and said, "I'll tell you later. Although right now I think we should stay here today. Give me another day to rest."

Kay looked over at him, smiling, and said, "That's a really great idea." They just sat around the fire all day, drinking coffee and talking.

Joe continued to avoid talking about the scars, and Kay finally gave up.

Kay started making supper when Joe got up and tried to roll a large log toward the camp. Kay ran over, saying, "Hey, what are you doing?"

Joe smiled and said, "Help me, and you'll see." A few minutes later, it was in place. About ten feet from the fire, Joe picked up his coffee and sat down with his back against the log. Kay smiled, grabbing hers, and sat next to him. Joe put his arm around her, pulling her a little closer.

Kay looked at him, saying, "I could spend the rest of my life right here with you."

He bent sideways and kissed her. Joe started looking around and spotted a birch tree about fifty feet away. It was about a foot in diameter. Then, looking at Kay, he said, "Honey, could you go over there and cut a strip of bark off that birch tree?" Then continuing, "Go as deep as you can about fourteen inches top   to bottom, all the way around." She looked at him funny and grabbed his hunting knife and headed for the tree.

She came back with the strip of bark and asked, "Okay. What's next?"

Joe said, "Help me."

He kneeled next to the log they had rolled closer to the fire. Holding his arm very carefully, Kay cut the strips, holding the sticks in place. Then Joe placed the bark around his arm, marking where to cut to make it fit.

Looking at Kay, he said, "Now put that in that big pot on the fire and fill it with water." Then he added, "After it warms up good, let it soak until it's pliable."

She got up and did what he asked, then came back and asked, "What are you up to?"

Joe smiled and said, "Making a cast for my arm."

She was still a little puzzled and asked, "How?"

Joe said, "When that bark is totally saturated with water, it's pliable. We can fit it to my arm and tie more strips off my old shirt. As it dries, it will shrink, making a stiff cast. It will be better support than those sticks."

About an hour later, she got the bark out of the warm water. Joe again kneeled by the log, supporting his arm. Kay carefully put the bark around his arm and wrapped the new cloth strips around it, and tied them. By late evening, the bark was dry, and Joe had a cast to support the broken bone.

Kay looked at him, smiling, and said, "Where on earth did you learn that?"

Laughing, he replied, "It's old Indian medicine. I was helping relocate some buffalo a long time ago. I spent a couple of weeks with some Indians in Wyoming. I sat and listened in the evening as they told stories of hunts. One of the stories was about a hundred years old. I listened to the old man as he talked about his grandfather getting run over by a big bull. The man suffered a broken arm. The medicine man of the tribe gave him something to drink made of dried flowers. It put him to sleep. While he was sleeping, he set the arm and put a birch bark cast on it. What was in that drink never came out and I didn't think to ask. Although I never forgot anything they talked about. They are very wise people."

Kay looked at him, simply amazed at what Joe had just said. She could not believe all the things he knew. Joe kept talking about natural cures.

He said, "The Indians have many cures that work, although they are not recognized by the Food and Drug Administration, so doctors can't tell you about them. Also, the large pharmaceutical companies don't want anyone to know about these. Think of the millions of dollars people could save by just walking out into the woods and making their own medicine."

Kay sat there listening. The more he talked, the more amazed she was. She had never heard of most of the things Joe had said.

Kay slowly got up and finished making supper. As she did, she thought about the things Joe had said.

Turning around, she asked, "Some are just plant extracts, right?"

Joe looked up and said, "Yes, absolutely, although you need to know what you are looking for." Joe then continued, "There are many all-natural cures for stuff like poison ivy, nettles, and mosquito bites. You can find these things growing wild in the woods." He then added, "There are even books you can buy that have the names and pictures with a very precise description of what you are looking for."

Kay and Joe sat by the campfire, eating their supper, and continued talking. Joe was a wealth of information. Suddenly, however, he stopped. She could tell he was thinking. Looking at Kay, he said, "That old Indian I listened to that night, he said one more thing that I never forgot." Kay just sat, waiting. He said, "May your fish always be larger than the holes in your net." Turning, he looked at her and said, "I only have one net. It's the one I threw over you. It's retired now. I'll never need to use it again."

Tears immediately came to Kay's eyes.

Looking at Joe, she said, "You won't ever need it again. There is no one on this planet who could ever take your place."

Joe smiled and said, "Let's clean up. I'm tired." Laughing, he added, "Healing is hard work."

As soon as everything was cleaned up, they walked down to the creek to clean themselves up. The water was getting colder every day. Joe knew they needed to get out of the mountains as soon as they could. He was starting to feel better, although he knew it was still a long walk.

As he stood, he said, "Don't move."

Kay froze.

She knew that tone and knew something was up. Joe slowly stepped in front of her. Then he said, "Okay, stand up and back up. Don't run. Walk backward and watch me."

Kay was not sure what was going on. Although when Joe's voice changed to the way he was talking now, she knew it was serious. She tried to look around him, and as she did, Joe said, "That's the biggest mountain lion I've ever seen!"

After walking backward about twenty yards, he stopped. Joe reached down and picked up a pretty stout branch.

As he did, Kay saw the cat. Kay took a deep breath and said, "Are we in the food chain?"

Joe smiled and said, "Not as a general rule, but a cat that big, not sure." Then he asked, "Do you have your pistol?" Kay said, "Aww, no, I don't."

He said, "Do you know where it is?"

She said, "Yes, next to yours on the log." Then she added, "So are both rifles."

"Okay," Joe said. "If that cat charges, I'm going to run at it, waving this club. You get to the guns as fast as you can."

They continued to walk backward, and the cat continued to walk toward them. With about fifty yards between them and the cat and only twenty to the camp, Joe told Kay, "Get a gun now and fire one shot into the ground. If that cat is on me, please don't miss." The cat was getting closer. Kay bolted for the guns, and Joe charged at the mountain lion.

As he ran, he yelled and waved his arms. Even with a sore leg, he moved quick enough to surprise the lion. It spun around and took four big leaps. As it did, Joe stopped, turned and walked as fast as he could toward the camp. Kay met him with both rifles. Joe grabbed his rifle, spun around, took aim, and fired. The 500-grain solid core bullet hit the ground about two feet in front of the mountain lion.

It spun around and headed for a safer area. Joe let out a deep breath.

Kay asked, "Did you miss on purpose?"

As Joe calmed down, he said, "Yes. I figured he had one warning shot. I was sure you had jacked a shell into yours just in case."

Kay said, "Yes. I was aiming at the cat when you shot. If it had come any closer, I would have shot it."

Joe looked at his wife. It was a comfort knowing she had his back at all times. He knew she was a fantastic shot. That was the biggest reason the cat was still alive. Alone or with anyone other than Kay, he would have had no choice but to kill it.

The sun had just dropped below the western mountains, and the valley they were in was full of shadows. Joe thought something did not feel right. He told Kay to get behind him. He did not know what it was, just that feeling of being uneasy. Looking around, he levered another round into his rifle. Then he pulled Kay up next to him. They walked very carefully back toward the camp.

The lion screamed as it jumped off the rock they were walking under. Joe swung, aimed, and fired in one blurry second. The cat dropped dead, not twenty feet away. Kay grabbed Joe, and together, they walked slowly toward the huge mountain lion. Joe poked it several times with his rifle. Then Kay and Joe walked toward the campfire and its comfort. Kay was a nervous mess. She was shaking and would not let Joe get more than a few feet away.

As he wrapped his arms around her, he could feel her shaking. So, he just held her, stroking her hair, saying, "Everything is fine." Then he whispered, "I told you I would always protect you. I'll never let anything hurt you, not ever."

Kay leaned back a little, looking into her husband's eyes. She could see the sincerity in his eyes and hear the surety in his voice. She knew without a doubt, if he could breathe, she knew she was safe.

They sat there talking for a few minutes. Then Kay stood up and walked over, taking both pistols. Then she headed to the tent. Joe watched her as she put the guns in their places. Then he looked at the fire. A few minutes later, he crawled into the tent, removed his clothes, and slid in next to Kay. It felt good to have his wife's body next to his. He pulled her close and kissed her. She would not let go and held him close long enough to feel his warmth and affection.

***

In the morning, Joe walked over to the cougar and looked at it. *What an amazing animal! It's too bad it made that last mistake.*

Joe knew the cat was a trophy, although he had no way of getting it out. In his condition, it was all he could do to just walk, let alone carry its hide and skull out. He pulled it under a rock over-hang and covered it with rocks. He thought it deserved to be buried.

He walked back to camp, and Kay had everything packed, and they started out.

The next two days went great.

As they walked, they talked or just enjoyed the peace and tranquility of this beautiful piece of the majestic Rocky Mountains of Northwest Montana. They could see sheer rock walls, tall snowcapped peaks, as well as miles of tree-covered slopes. They would stop for a minute to admire the beauty of this wild yet wonderful area.

Every night since the mountain lion attack, Kay stayed close to Joe. They both carried their pistols everywhere. As Kay was making supper, Joe kept walking around, gathering firewood. Kay watched him continuously, never letting him out of her sight. She was still thinking about how fast he had reacted to the lion. She replayed it over and over in her mind. It felt like she heard the cat scream as it died. His natural hunting instincts were unbelievable. She watched him as he walked back, limping just a little, carrying way too much wood. She thought, *He really is a mountain man. He's more at home here than in our home in Chicago.*

In the morning, they got loaded up and headed out again. Joe was feeling better every day. Late that afternoon, they came to another river. This one was too wide and deep for them to cross, and the water was running way too fast to even try. Joe stood on the bank, looking upstream and downstream. They made camp there.

As Kay made supper, Joe walked upstream, looking for a place to cross. He got back just as she had everything ready. She looked at Joe, saying, "So what do you think? I know we can't cross that."

Joe said, "I walked upstream about half a mile. It doesn't shrink much, and that current is way too fast. I think we'll have to go upstream to find a place. Hopefully, a shallow area where we can walk across."

Kay asked, "Why upstream? Wouldn't it be easier to go downstream?"

Joe said, "Rivers get wider the farther downstream they go. We might have to cross a couple of smaller ones, then it should get narrow enough for us to cross."

They got a really early start the next day, and about noon, they came to the end of the trail. A sheer rock wall about twenty feet tall. Joe looked at Kay and said, "Damn, honey. I think we are in trouble."

She said, "You're the mountain man. What are we going

to do?"

Joe, looking around, said, "Climb that cliff and go cross-country. As long as we keep heading west, we will come out somewhere eventually."

Kay looked up the cliff, saying, "Who's climbing that? Not me!"

Joe laughed, saying, "I'll lead. We'll be roped together." Looking at the rope they had, he added, "I think we have enough."

Kay asked, "What about the horse?"

Joe looked at the horse, saying, "He knows the way home alone. He can cross the river somewhere, and he'll probably beat us there."

She looked at the horse, then their shrinking supplies, and knew what they were going to do. They could pack everything now. They would burn everything except what they needed to survive. This was Joe at his best, surviving with nothing and coming out on top. She knew if she did what he said, they would walk out of the mountains within a mile of the truck.

After dinner, they started going through what was left. Anything that would burn went into the fire. After sorting and resorting, they had two packs of everything they would need to survive in the mountains for four or five days. They were sure they would be out by then.

In the morning, Kay made breakfast and coffee. It was

faster than usual, although Kay did slip Joe some painkiller. She knew he would overdo it that day. Joe turned the horse loose and slapped him on the rump. He took off running down the valley in the wrong direction. Joe just looked and said, "Hey, buddy, home is that way!"

He and Kay then walked to the rock wall. Joe was looking for a really easy route. They would be free climbing. They would be tied together, but Joe knew if one of them slipped, they would probably both die.

Joe found what he was looking for. It had a little bit of a slope. They took off their packs and rifles, and Joe took the longest rope and tied everything together. He tied that rope around himself. Then he took the shorter rope and tied himself and Kay together.

He said, "Put on those light, tight leather gloves. Those should protect your hands from the sharp edges." He gave Kay a hug and a kiss and added, "Follow me. Try to stay about fifteen feet or less behind me. We can do this. It's not that tall."

As they climbed, Joe kept looking under his arm at Kay. She was doing great, staying about ten feet behind him, watching where he put his hands and feet, climbing like she had done it all her life.

Joe, reaching the top, rolled over and was getting up when he heard Kay scream. He dove forward, grabbing a tree just as the rope tried jerking him backward. Kay was still screaming as he dug in, and using everything he had, he pulled her up. He got around the tree and, still pulling her up, he got back to the cliff edge.

Kay was hanging about four feet below him, trying to get a hold of something. As she was swinging back and forth, Joe noticed the rope was on a sharp piece of stone. Every time she moved; it would cut a little more.

Joe reached over the edge and said, "Kay, grab my wrist just above my glove."

Kay swung and grabbed Joe's wrist. As he tried to lift her, he could feel his grip slipping. He was also watching the rope cut.

Quietly and calmly, he looked at Kay, saying, "Honey, Kay, honey, look at me. You're going to be okay. Now, honey, please reach up with your other hand and grab my arm. Kay, honey, you can do this."

She swung, but couldn't quite grab Joe's arm. Every time she swung; the rope cut a little more.

Looking at her, he said, "Kay, make one hard swing and grab my arm." He was as calm as he could be, knowing the rope would cut through at any minute. She made two more swings, and as she completed the second one, she had Joe's arm just above her other hand. She gripped it tight; the rope had cut through. Joe looked at his wife, and taking a deep breath, he started lifting her. As she came over the edge, he got his arm around her. Falling backward, he pulled Kay over the edge. They collapsed on the cliff, holding each other. They were both crying and holding on.

Kay said, "I thought I was dead."

Joe said, "As the rope cut through, I thought I had lost you. Then I felt your hand grab my arm. At that point, all I could do was lift and try to drag you over the edge."

They lay there, just holding each other. Joe had tears running out of his eyes. Kay was still crying and held Joe so tight he could hardly breathe. But he did not care. He had Kay in his arms, and that was all that mattered.

After they lay there together, holding, hugging, and kissing each other, Joe rolled over and asked, "Should we build a cabin here or go back to Chicago?"

Kay sat up and looked at what Joe was looking at.

She smiled, wiping the tears from her eyes, and said, "Oh, my, that's beautiful!"

They could see for miles down a long, narrow valley.

She turned and looked at Joe, saying, "Let's move out here somewhere in a few years."

Joe's eyes shot wide open, and he said, "Really? You want to move out here? Really? Wow, absolutely! You know we do have my cabin. It's about a hundred and fifty miles south of here." As he grabbed her again, he whispered, "Home is any place you are, and that's all I care about."

Joe reached and grabbed the rope and started pulling their packs up. As they got close, Kay reached for them. She grabbed them, and Joe grabbed her belt, just to make sure she did not get pulled over the edge. They got their packs on, grabbed their rifles, and headed out, walking in a western direction.

Kay could tell Joe was sore. She weighed about 120 pounds, and Joe had lifted her with one arm, then grabbed her and pulled her to safety. He was right; as long as he was alive, she would never be hurt.

They hiked all day. The going was slow and steep, but they still managed to make a good distance. Joe figured about ten miles total, not including the first climb.

They made camp, had a fast supper, and crawled into their sleeping bags. They were both dead tired. Kay was sore, and she knew Joe was, too. To make matters worse, they were out of the powered painkiller.

In the morning, they had coffee and a quick breakfast, and off they went. They walked into a canyon, and Joe looked at the climb, remembering the day before. They then backtracked and found an easier climb just about as steep, only there were trees and bushes to hold on to. At the top, they rested for an hour. Joe reached over and kissed Kay on the cheek.

She looked at him and said, "What was that for?"

He smiled, saying, "Because I can."

She laughed and dove onto him. As they fell over backward, he spun just enough so she would land on top.

They laughed as Joe tickled her, rolling away.

She punched him in the arm and said, "I want a hot shower and a soft bed, so, Mr. Mountain Man, find me one."

Joe looked at her and said, "Your wish is my command." They got up, walked for three more hours, and came out into a field where they could see the lights of a house. As they walked across the field, they heard children playing. Joe had brought her out to safety.

The family in the house let them use their phone book and phone. Joe called his friend who lived there and gave him the address, and half an hour later, they were headed to his place, where a hot shower and soft bed awaited them.

After they got cleaned up, they sat and talked half the night, drinking beer and laughing. Calvin and his wife, Kelley, could not believe the story they heard. Calvin had known Joe since they were kids and knew he could survive in the woods. Although this was amazing. A true to life story about survival in the wilderness.

At about 1:00 a.m., they all headed to bed.

As Kay crawled into bed next to Joe, she slowly reached for him, kissing him gently. Joe could smell her perfume.

She's all mine.

Taking her into his arms, he rolled her over and started kissing her.

Late the next morning, they went to where they had rented the horses to talk to the owner. He said, "Yeah, all four had come back the day before. I was a little worried when the last two showed up. I figured I would call the sheriff today."

They talked about the lost tack, saddles, and bridles that were left in the mountains. They made a deal, and the four friends headed to town.

Coffee and breakfast first, then a trip to the doctor's office. Joe kept saying he was okay, although Kay knew he was hurting. After a good checkup, including x-rays of his arm and leg to make sure there was nothing in it, the doctor said, "You did an excellent job, and he should be just fine in a couple of weeks."

He then called in a prescription for antibiotics, and off they went to pick it up.

Joe and Kay stayed with Calvin and Kelly for two more days while Joe rested. They had a few bottles of beer in the evening and talked, laughed, and joked with each other. Every night, when they crawled into bed, Kay made Joe realize how lucky he really was.

On the third morning out of the mountains, Joe said, "I think we better take off tomorrow. Let's go to the airport today and check over our plane. We can load some of our gear up to make it easier tomorrow."

Joe and Calvin left for the airport while Kay and Kelly stayed at the house and washed the rest of the clothes they did not throw away. The four went out for dinner and drinks after. Joe and Calvin got a bit loaded, and Kelly drove home.

They sat around talking longer, knowing it might be a year or more before they would see each other again.

Joe told Calvin to keep his eyes open and that Kay wanted to move to somewhere in that area in a few years.

Calvin said, "There's a house for sale just a couple of miles away."

Kay said, "Oh, no, you two cannot live that close. You'll be in trouble way too often." That got everyone laughing.

Kelly looked up and said, "Absolutely, not a chance!"

After coffee in the morning, Calvin and Kelly drove Kay and Joe to the airport. While Kay went inside to use the restroom, Joe started the preflight inspection and triple checked everything. Calvin stood watching. After Joe was done, he asked a few questions, and they started walking inside as Kay and Kelly came walking out. Calvin stopped with them as Joe continued inside.

As he walked out, Calvin yelled, "Hey, Joe, your wife just kissed me!"

Joe said, "What? I missed that."

"Aw, crap," said Calvin, laughing.

The four friends stood there, talking a while longer as they slowly walked toward the plane. Kay gave Kelly and Calvin a hug as Joe hugged Kelly. He grabbed Calvin, and the two men looked at each other. It was that look of lifelong friends. You don't say a thing, and the other knows what you're saying. It's in the eyes.

Joe helped Kay step on the wing over the flaps and get in. Shaking Calvin's hand again, Joe got in and shut and locked the door. Reaching over, he locked Kay's, switched on the fuel pumps, and watching the pressure climb, hit the starter. Engine one fired and started. Switching on the second pump, he watched the pressure and started engine two. Checking all gauges, he called air traffic control and waited for clearance to taxi.

They waved to Calvin and Kelly again, and Joe pushed the throttles forward as the plane rolled. He was cleared to runway thirty-four and told to hold long. A 727 was inbound, and the wing vortex would blow toward them. While waiting, he explained to Kay what a wing vortex was and why it was dangerous to a small plane. He explained it was like a sideways tornado and could flip the plane if not handled correctly. Kay looked at Joe and said, "You're kidding, right?"

Just then, the 727 went past them.

As the vortex hit the 310, Kay grabbed the dash and said, "Wow, what was that?"

Joe smiled, saying, "Vortex."

Chapter Fourteen

As he was cleared to take off, Joe pushed the throttles forward, set the props to take off, and pulled the 310 into the air.

Reaching over, he lifted the flaps and gear and wiggled the wings as they headed for home.

After, they stopped at Butte to top the tanks and use the restrooms. Joe taxied out and cleared to takeoff; he again pushed the throttles forward and reached over, kissing Kay. He lifted the flaps and gear, tipped the 310 into a turn to the southeast. As they climbed, he started feeling sick. He quickly trimmed the plane to climb and sat back, trying to relax.

As they climbed through twelve thousand feet, Kay asked, "How high are we going?"

Joe looked at her and said, "I think we'll climb to 13,500. Then I'll set the autopilot and let this take us to Sheridan, Wyoming."

She smiled and said, "Honey, are you feeling alright?"

Joe looked at Kay, saying, "I'm not sure. I feel a little sick." Then he said, "Kay, take the controls. I want you to know how to keep this thing level."

As she reached for the controls, he switched off the autopilot. The plane started descending. He said, pull back just a little and use this switch to readjust the trim to level the flight." As she played with the controls and trim control, Joe said, "You are doing great."

Kay flew the plane while Joe tried to relax. She looked over at him and said, "Joe, you don't look good. What's wrong, honey?"

Joe said, "I'm not sure. I feel really strange."

Kay kept the plane level and going straight. Joe looked at the GPS. Realizing they were getting close to Sheridan, he reached over and started setting up the descent into Sheridan. Calling air traffic, he informed them he was the only pilot on board and was sick. He asked for a straight-in approach and landing clearance. He set up the instrument landing system and told Kay she was doing great.

He said, "Watch those two needles in front of you. Try to keep them crossed in the center like they are now."

Joe kept pulling the power back and the props forward, so if they needed to do an aborted landing, all he had to do was push the throttles to full power. He hoped he could fly by then.

As they came in a little fast, he dropped the flaps and gear, thus slowing the plane, and made a little steeper descent. Joe took the plane as they were crossing the outer markers, landed, pulled the power to an idle, and taxied off the runway and started throwing up. The medical personnel were already there. He was trying to clean up as they opened the door, and he rolled out of the plane, dropped to the ground, and started vomiting again.

At the hospital, they figured he had a reaction to the antibiotics and pumped fluid into him. A couple of hours later, they released him. Joe and Kay got a motel room that night. Joe called the airport. That was when they told him Kay had taxied the plane and tied it down. He looked at Kay.

She smiled, saying, "I've watched you enough. It wasn't that hard."

Joe looked at his wife again. He knew how lucky he was.

Joe and Kay both ate a very light supper. Joe was still a little sick. Kay was a little nervous and scared. She watched him very closely, making sure he was okay. They got back to the motel, took showers, and headed to bed. Kay snuggled close to Joe. She put her arm under his pillow and the other against his chest. He had one propped up against the headboard and the other around Kay.

As he drifted off to sleep, he dreamed about crashing airplanes, grizzly bears, and mountain lions. In the morning, he did not know why, but all he wanted to do was lie there holding Kay as long as she would lay still.

All he knew was that having her there was the greatest feeling he could ever hope to have. They stayed in Sheridan for an extra day. Joe had been through the wringer. He was still sore and stiff. The extra time lying around would not hurt either of them. They walked around town, did a little shopping, and spent time sitting in the hot tub.

They went wheels up the next day and flew to Iowa, spending two days with Kay's family. She was in heaven with her grandkids around. She loved her children and grandkids. They were her life until she met Joe. They still were. Joe just filled the gap right under them.

He said, "I'll never be number one in your life, but I can live with that. As long as I'm number two, right under your grandkids, I'll always be happy."

After three days there, they flew home. Kay flew most of the way.

Joe wanted her to learn. She thought it was a lot of fun. They got clearance to land and fueled the plane. As they started unloading the airplane, Kay said, "I think we must have forgotten about half of our camping supplies in Montana. I think the plane is considerably lighter than going out?"

Joe chuckled as he put the last of their camping supplies in the pickup and said, "Yeah, it sure looks that way."

Together, they pushed the plane into the hangar.

Walking to Kay, he put his arms around her. Looking at the plane, he said, "We're nearly home. We're alive and you're safe. Let's go home and get a couple of days of doing absolutely nothing."

Kay smiled. Looking into his eyes, she replied, "You are an amazing man, and I love you. Let's go home."

They slept in the following morning.

Joe slowly slipped out of bed and headed for the shower.

Coming out wrapped in a towel, he met Kay at the door. She reached over and took his t-shirt and said, "I've seen the scars and bullet wounds. I'm going to make coffee and we are going to talk about this. I'm your wife, and I need to know what happened and when. I also want to know if you have any other secrets you haven't told me."

Joe turned, walking into their room. He finished getting dressed and headed for the kitchen and a waiting Kay.

Sitting down, he said, "There are parts of my past you can't know about. It's for your own safety. You have to trust me on this."

Kay looked into the eyes of the man she thought she knew better than anyone on this planet and said, "My safety? Really? If it's so damn dangerous to be around you, then why did you keep seeing me?"

Joe replied through tear-filled eyes, "Because I couldn't imagine my life without you."

Kay stood and said, "You have saved my life twice. I saved yours once. I'm sorry to say but that's as close as we are ever going to get. If you can't level with me, maybe you had better leave!"

Standing, Joe looked at Kay and said, "I love you more than life."

He turned and he dumped his coffee in the sink and walked out.

Getting in his pickup, he drove away.

Kay ran into the bedroom and fell onto the bed, crying. She cried all day. Several times, she picked up the phone to call. But changed her mind and put it down.

She called her daughters but never mentioned the fact that she had pushed Joe into a corner, and he had walked out. She called work to tell them she was home but would be taking a few more days off.

Digging through Joe's desk, she found Logan's number. Sitting there, she stared at the number until she called.

Logan answered on the first ring, saying, "Hey Joe. How was your trip into the Bob Marshal?"

Kay answered, saying, "Sorry, Logan, this is Kay. Joe and I got into a fight. I kind of pushed him into a corner. I told him if he couldn't level with me, maybe he should leave." Kay's voice started to break up, and she paused. Taking a deep breath, she continued, "Logan, he left. What the hell did I do? I love him so much. I have some questions for you. Joe got hurt and we spent a couple of days healing. I, ummm, he, ummm. Aww shit. I shouldn't have called. He had a really high fever. I've felt the scars on him before although I had never seen them. I had to try and cool him down. I cut away his shirt and saw them. Do you know how or where he got them? There are also bullet wounds. Hell! He has been shot several times. Not to mention cut with something like he's been tortured."

Logan took a deep breath and said, "Yes, I do. Although, I'm sworn to secrecy. I don't know everything, but I do know this. He would never have married you if he thought he couldn't protect you. I know he loves you. Give him a day or two and he'll be back, and I bet you two talk. That's all I can say although I'm going to call him."

Kay said between sobs, "Are you sure he'll be back? I don't want him to leave."

Logan replied, "Yes, I'm quite sure he'll be back. I'm betting by tomorrow. Just let him think. You know how he is under pressure. He'll come to the right conclusion."

Still crying, Kay said, "God, I hope so. If you hear from him, call me. Please."

Logan replied, "Absolutely. I'll be calling you within an hour or so."

Kay said, "Thanks, Logan. Talk to you soon." Breaking the call, she walked into the living room, sat down on the couch and started crying again.

***

Joe drove around for a couple of hours, thinking. Seeing a motel, he got a room. Sitting on the edge of the bed, he called Logan just to disconnect before it went through.

Getting up, he walked into the bathroom and looked into the mirror, saying, "Okay, Randy or Robert or whoever the hell you are. Now what are you going to do? You love her and you started this mess, so how are you going to fix it?"

Staring at himself in the mirror, he shook his head and swore loud enough to be heard a couple of blocks away.

Picking up his phone, he found Kay's number and stared at it. Scrolling further, he found Logan's and hit call.

Logan answered on the first ring, saying, "Hey you. How was your trip into the Bob Marshal?"

Joe replied, "We had a great time if you think having a pack of wolves chasing off the horses and nearly getting killed trying to walk out is a good time."

"You're kidding, right?"

"Nope, not at all."

"Are you home now?"

"Aww, kind of."

"What do you mean kind of? You're either home or you're not."

"Kay and I got into a fight, and I walked out. She saw all my scars and wants to know where and how. Damn Logan, I'm not sure I can protect her. I sure can't tell her everything. Logan, I killed two of what I think were MS13 members last summer at my cabin in Montana. They were looking for Randy Jackson. They asked for him by name. I took their bodies way back up into the mountains and put the climbing gear on them. Tied them together and threw them off a cliff. If someone ever finds them, they'll think it's a climbing accident. I need to sell that cabin. I need you to list it and be my agent. I have to stay out of Montana for a while. They are still looking for me out there. They know I've lived out there most of my life."

"Absolutely. I'll do whatever you need. But you need to do something for me, also. I know you have a very dark past. But now you need to open to Kay and tell her enough to make her happy and keep her in your life. Joe, you need her. I've known you a long time, and I've never seen you this happy."

Joe let out a deep sigh. "Yeah, I know. Let me think about how much to tell her, and I'll call her later."

Joe sat on the edge of the bed deep in thought. *What can I do? How much can I tell her? I still have a price on my head by the Taliban and the Colombians.*

Laying down, he continued to think and slowly, he decided he had to level with her so she can make the decision. After all, it's her life. If he tells her everything, she can weigh the odds and decide.

Laying there, he was satisfied that he was doing the right thing. But now he was worried that she'll think it's too dangerous to be around him. Silently, he said a quiet prayer as he slowly drifted off.

***

Kay got up and walked to the window, looking for Joe's pickup.

Watching a car drive by, she checked the doors and walked slowly into bed. Laying down, she started to cry again and cried herself to sleep.

***

Joe suddenly jerked wide awake. Something was wrong. It was the same feeling he'd gotten several times before. Getting out of bed, he looked out the window. Pacing back and forth, he couldn't take it anymore. Quickly, he got dressed and, looking at his watch, he headed for Kay's. He's had this feeling so many times, and it's always meant danger.

Parking two blocks away, Joe quickly opened the glove box. Seeing two pieces of copper wire, he put them in his pocket. He slipped into the shadows, and as quietly as a light breeze, he headed for Kay's.

Sitting in the shadow of a large tree, he watched as someone walked across the yard towards the house. Slowly, he circled around the other way to come up from behind. Noticing the guy's pants were too big and baggy, held up by a belt.

In his left hand, he held an MK3 naval, military knife with a blade lying flat against his arm. A .45 was in a holster clipped to his belt in the center of his back. Slipping from shadow to shadow, he came up on the guy looking in the bedroom window.

Putting his right hand over his mouth, he sliced through the guy's belt, letting his pants fall to the ground. Then, he drove his right into the guy's stomach just below his ribs and came up with a bone jarring left, still holding the knife into his jaw. The man let out a muffled moan as the air left his lungs and the left connected. His eyes rolled up and down he went.

Joe grabbed the wire and dropped the knife point first into the ground. Taking the three feet of bare copper wire, he made two quick wraps around each wrist and twisted the ends.

With one down, he slipped back into the shadows and starts looking for the second while hoping there were only two. Working his way back into the shadows, he waited. Seeing the second guy walking around the house, Joe slipped up to the corner of the house and dropped to his knees.

As the second idiot came around the corner, Joe drove a hard left into his balls. Then, standing up, he grabbed a handful of hair as he unleashed a left uppercut. Connecting solidly with the guy's jaw, he let the guy go as he sank to the ground.

Grabbing his hair and an arm, he pulled him to a standing position and lifted him into a fireman's carry and hauled him across the road to a vacant lot. There, he took the wire and with a wraparound on both wrists, he pulled up one, and binds all three together.

Walking back but still staying in the shadows, he found idiot number one just coming to. Joe took the knife and laid it across his throat, whispering, "If you say so much as a squeak, I'll cut your throat and drop you at the dump where the rats can eat you. Do you understand me?"

The guy's eyes opened wide as he felt the knife against his throat and very carefully nodded his head. Joe pulled him to his feet, and together, they walked across the road while remaining in the shadows. Joe pulled him around and with his hand still wrapped around the hilt of the knife; he drove his fist into the guy's jaw. With a right hook following, the idiot went limp and dropped.

Joe untied the wire and tied the first idiot about the same as the other. Walking back to his pickup, he waited and watched as the sun slowly changed the night sky.

After an hour and not seeing anyone else, he pulled forward into Kay's driveway and walked to the door. Not sure if he should walk in or not, he knocked.

Kay was walking out of the bedroom when she heard the knock.

Chapter Fifteen

Opening the door, she stood frozen in place as Joe handed her a huge bouquet of roses and said, "We need to talk."

Kay replied, "You don't need to knock. Remember, you live here."

Joe smiled as Kay took the flowers and said, "I sure hope so. But after you hear what I'm about to tell you. I might have to find somewhere else to live."

Kissing her cheek, he walked in and sat down.

Looking at Kay, he said, "Come here, honey. Now please don't ask any questions until I'm done. Then I'll answer any and all of the questions you have."

Kay put the flowers in a vase and poured two cups of coffee. Walking over to Joe, she said, "If you don't want to tell me, you don't have to. I talked to Logan and although he didn't really tell me anything, he said I should just trust you. Then an hour later, Colton called. I'm sure Logan called him. Anyway, he told me a lot of your past is still classified. Which means no one is supposed to know about it. Right? So, if you're going to tell me anything, then please only tell me what you legally can. Oh, and one more thing Joe." Pausing, she took a deep breath and said, "Last night was the worst night of my life. I missed you, and I didn't know it was possible to hurt that bad. I think even a phone call would have helped. I don't think I slept at all. I don't ever want another night like that. I just want you in my life as much as possible. Plus, the fact there's not another man that could ever take your place. I feel like I have found the man God put on earth for me. Joe, I love you more than I ever dreamed possible."

Joe sat there with tears in his eyes as he listened to what she had to say. Then, taking a deep breath, he replied, "You saw me shoot. I was a sniper in the military. What I did was simple. I hunted down and killed Taliban members, their helpers, and informants. I was in Iraq, Iran, and Afghanistan. I spent over four years killing for our government."

Pausing, he took a sip of coffee and started again by saying, "Joe is not my given birth name. I was named Randy by my parents. I'm not going to tell you my last name as of yet. I probably should not have told you my first name, but it's too late now. After Afghanistan, I went to work for the DEA. I was a deep undercover agent and operative for ten years. I did pretty much the same in the jungles of Colombia that I did in the mountains of Afghanistan. Only I was killing drug lords, the leaders of the cocaine cartel, and their members. I was also causing as much hate and discontent between the cartels as possible. I spent just over ten years in Colombia. I stayed until they found me, and I had to leave. The Taliban and the cocaine cartels both have a price on my head. I'm probably the most hated man in both countries."

Standing, Joe walked across the kitchen and picked up a

box of Kleenex. Taking one out, he hands it to Kay and put the box down. Then, filling both coffee cups and his water glass, he sat down and said, "I was finally captured in Colombia. I ran from them for three days. When they caught me, I killed the first two and seriously injured at least one more before overwhelming numbers won."

Standing, he pulled his t-shirt over his head. Kay's eyes grew as she actually saw the scars for the first time. When they were in Montana, she was looking through tear-filled eyes most of the time.

Standing, she walked around the table and placed her hand on Joe's chest and slowly traced the knife wounds. Closing her eyes, she saw him hanging from the ceiling as they beat and tortured him.

Slowly, she walked behind him, and tears came again. They poured from her eyes like rain as she traced the ones on his back and felt the bullet wounds. As Kay came the rest of the way around, he pulled out a chair and she sat down.

Joe reached and grabbed a handful of Kleenex and said, "When I got loose, I killed at least two before running. I ran for Bogota and the US Embassy. That was the only place I thought might help me. On the last day, as I was nearing the embassy, they caught up with me again. In the running fight that took place, I killed several more before being shot five more times and falling through the gate to safety. The marines on duty opened fire and saved my life."

Stopping, he looked around and reached for more Kleenex. Handing them to her, he took a sip of coffee and said, "I'm now in the witness protection program. Only the judge that helped set it up about six years ago has been murdered and my only trusted contact with the DEA has retired. So, I'm pretty much on my own."

Standing, he walked to the window. Looking out, he took another sip of coffee. He stopped and got a glass of water before sitting down and saying, "My cover was blown just over six years ago. I killed two men in my apartment that night. I called my handler and told him. He wanted me to come in. I said no way. I didn't trust him or anyone he was involved with. I know there was a leak on the inside. A few days later, I called a very close friend who I was in the service with. He also worked for the DEA. Only he was a captain. He talked to a federal judge and set up a total new me. The Joe West you fell in love with."

Taking a sip of coffee, then a drink of water, he said, "That brings us up to a few years ago. The night I met you, I just knew you were the only woman in the world for me. It was the look in your eyes and the feeling in my heart. I sat in my room the next day and thought about just leaving. Kay, I don't know if I can protect you from all of this. Last summer, while we were in Montana, that last morning when I went back up to the cabin, there were two guys there. They asked me if I knew Randy. I played stupid, but I think they knew it was me because as I offered to shake hands, one pulled a knife. I killed both of them. That's when I found out the judge had been murdered and Adrian retired. I don't have any other number for Adrian, and I have no idea where he is."

Pausing again, he looked into Kay's eyes and said, "I've told you about as much as I can for now. There are a lot of things you need to decide. All I can say is as long as I'm breathing, I'll make sure no one ever harms you in any way. Oh, by the way, there were a couple of idiots sneaking around last night. Both are across the road, hog-tied and lying in the empty lot. When I left, they were unconscious. "

Kay's eyes flew open as she said, "What? Who? Where?" Pausing, she slowed down and said, "What happened? Who's unconscious? Where are they? Are they, umm, dead?"

Joe said, "Please, Kay, calm down and listen. I saw two guys sneaking around, looking in the windows. They are both hog-tied and in the empty lot across the road, very much alive, just out cold when I left. I'm not sure if l should call the cops or not. I don't want any police involvement. I'm not sure how far they can dig and I, umm, I don't want the publicity. Now you have a lot to think about. Am I worth the risk that comes with me? I'm going to take care of those two idiots. I won't kill them. Then I'm going back to the motel. Call me later and let me know what your decision is. Otherwise, I'll start moving my stuff tomorrow."

Kay sat there, watching as Joe opened the door and left

without a backwards glance. Slipping on her robe, she followed him to the end of the driveway. Watching as he reached down and cut the two guys loose and took their picture, saying, "I'm not going to call the police. However, if ever see either of you again. They'll never find your bodies. Now get out of here and don't ever come back."

Both guys tried to hold up their pants as they walked towards the road. Seeing Kay, the one guy nodded and said in Spanish, "Wow, look at her. What I wouldn't give for a couple of hours alone."

From behind, Joe answered him in Spanish, "Are you really looking for a slow death? That's my wife you're talking about."

They both stopped and turned around. Looking at Joe, they say this time in English, "I didn't think you would understand me."

Joe replied, "Just get out of here before I change my mind and need to find a place to dump your worthless asses."

Both guys left at a jog as Joe walked back to Kay and said, "See, they're not dead. Although I think they should be. They were speaking in Spanish. I can understand, speak, and write in Spanish perfectly. Ten years in Colombia."

Pausing, he watched as the two idiots got into a car and drove away. Looking at Kay, he said, "You need to think if it's you and me or us. Do I have to run again or stand and fight to protect us?"

Kay took a step forward and wrapped her arm around him, saying, "I'm your wife. I know you'll always do your best to protect me. You have proven that over and over. There is no need for you to leave here this morning or ever. Just come home and love me."

Together, they walked back into the house and locked the door.

Epilogue

Three thousand miles away, Hector Ortiz was reading an online news reel when he saw a picture of a woman and a guy standing next to a Cessna 310. The article was about how Joe West—a big game guide, professional hunter, wildlife trapping and relocating wildlife expert, and wildlife biologists—rescues his wife—Kay West; the managing editor for Chicago Women's magazine—in Alaska when a plane she was in crashed in the Rangel St Elias mountains of South East Alaska. Then when the two took a vacation in Montana only to have their horses chased off by a pack of wolves. Suffering a broken arm—which the two set themselves in the wilderness—and then having a huge gash torn in his leg while crossing a flooded stream. Staying in a snow cave overnight to wait out a blizzard. He still managed to walk nearly fifty miles to lead them safely out of the wilderness.

Hector went back to the picture. Clicking on it, he expanded it just to get a better look at her. Seeing just how beautiful the lady really was, he called to Juan and said, "Get over here. We need to contact this guy. Look at his wife. She would bring a fortune on the market. With her looks and body, those Asians would go nuts bidding on her. Plus, the fact they own that plane. It's probably worth somewhere between $100,000 and $300,000. If we worked it right. We could end up with several hundred thousand dollars each. Think ransom her to him for $500,000 then simply kill him. Dump his body in the desert and sell her anyway. She could bring another two, maybe $300,000. Look at that body. She is all woman. I think maybe I will keep her myself for a while."

Juan replied, "Oh man, absolutely. Do you think we can get them into Mexico somehow?"

Hector looked at the article again and replied, "Wildlife trapping and relocating expert."

Juan looked over Hector's shoulder and replied, "Get started."

To be continued.